IBS

Books by Isaac Bashevis Singer

NOVELS

THE MANOR

I. THE MANOR II. THE ESTATE

THE FAMILY MOSKAT THE MAGICIAN OF LUBLIN

SATAN IN GORAY THE SLAVE

ENEMIES, A LOVE STORY

SHOSHA

STORIES

A FRIEND OF KAFKA GIMPEL THE FOOL SHORT FRIDAY

THE SÉANCE THE SPINOZA OF MARKET STREET

A CROWN OF FEATHERS PASSIONS

MEMOIRS

IN MY FATHER'S COURT

FOR CHILDREN

A DAY OF PLEASURE THE FOOLS OF CHELM

MAZEL AND SHLIMAZEL OR THE MILK OF A LIONESS

WHEN SHLEMIEL WENT TO WARSAW A TALE OF THREE WISHES

ELIJAH THE SLAVE WHY NOAH CHOSE THE DOVE

JOSEPH AND KOZA OR THE SACRIFICE TO THE VISTULA

ALONE IN THE WILD FOREST THE WICKED CITY

NAFTALI THE STORYTELLER AND HIS HORSE, SUS

COLLECTION

AN ISAAC BASHEVIS SINGER READER

The Spinoza of Market Street

Isaac Bashevis Singer

Farrar, Straus and Giroux
New York

Library of Congress catalog card number 61–13676

"Shiddah and Kuziba" and "The Man Who Came Back" first appeared in Commentary; "The Beggar Said So" and "The Spinoza of Market Street" in Esquire; "A Piece of Advice" in Hadassah Newsletter; "The Shadow of a Crib" in Mademoiselle; "In the Poorhouse" in Midstream; "A Tale of Two Liars" in Noonday 1; and "Black Wedding" in Noonday 3

Published simultaneously in Canada. Manufactured in the United States of America. Designed by Marshall Lee

Seventh printing, 1979

Contents

The Spinoza of Market Street

I

Dr. Nahum Fischelson paced back and forth in his garret room in Market Street, Warsaw. Dr. Fischelson was a short, hunched man with a grayish beard, and was quite bald except for a few wisps of hair remaining at the nape of the neck. His nose was as crooked as a beak and his eyes were large, dark, and fluttering like those of some huge bird. It was a hot summer evening, but Dr. Fischelson wore a black coat which reached to his knees, and he had on a stiff collar and a bow tie. From the door he paced slowly to the dormer window set high in the slanting room and back again. One had to mount several steps to look out. A candle in a brass holder was burning on the table and a variety of insects buzzed around the flame. Now and again one of the creatures would fly too close to the fire and sear its wings, or one would ignite and glow on the wick for an instant. At such moments Dr. Fischelson grimaced. His wrinkled face would twitch and beneath his disheveled moustache he would bite his lips. Finally he took a handkerchief from his pocket and waved it at the insects.

"Away from there, fools and imbeciles," he scolded. "You won't get warm here; you'll only burn yourself."

The insects scattered but a second later returned and once more circled the trembling flame. Dr. Fischelson wiped the sweat from his wrinkled forehead and sighed, "Like men they desire nothing but the pleasure of the moment." On the table lay an open book written in Latin, and on its broad-margined pages were notes and comments printed in small letters by Dr. Fischelson. The book was Spinoza's *Ethics* and Dr. Fischelson had been studying it for the last thirty years. He knew every proposition, every proof, every corollary, every note by heart. When he wanted to find a particular passage, he generally opened to the place immediately without having to search for it. But, nevertheless, he continued to study the *Ethics* for hours every day with a magnifying glass in his bony hand, murmuring and nodding his head in agreement. The truth was that the more Dr. Fischelson studied, the more puzzling sentences, unclear passages, and cryptic remarks he found. Each sentence contained hints unfathomed by any of the students of Spinoza. Actually the philosopher had anticipated all of the criticisms of pure reason made by Kant and his followers. Dr. Fischelson was writing a commentary on the *Ethics*. He had drawers full of notes and drafts, but it didn't seem that he would ever be able to complete his work. The stomach ailment which had plagued him for years was growing worse from day to day.

Now he would get pains in his stomach after only a few mouthfuls of oatmeal. "God in Heaven, it's difficult, very difficult," he would say to himself using the same intonation as had his father, the late Rabbi of Tishevitz. "It's very, very hard."

Dr. Fischelson was not afraid of dying. To begin with, he was no longer a young man. Secondly, it is stated in the fourth part of the *Ethics* that "a free man thinks of nothing less than of death and his wisdom is a meditation not of death, but of life." Thirdly, it is also said that "the human mind cannot be absolutely destroyed with the human body but there is some part of it that remains eternal." And yet Dr. Fischelson's ulcer (or perhaps it was a cancer) continued to bother him. His tongue was always coated. He belched frequently and emitted a different foul-smelling gas each time. He suffered from heartburn and cramps. At times he felt like vomiting and at other times he was hungry for garlic, onions, and fried foods. He had long ago discarded the medicines prescribed for him by the doctors and had sought his own remedies. He found it beneficial to take grated radish after meals and lie on his bed, belly down, with his head hanging over the side. But these home remedies offered only temporary relief. Some of the doctors he consulted insisted there was nothing the matter with him. "It's just nerves," they told him. "You could live to be a hundred."

But on this particular hot summer night, Dr. Fischelson felt his strength ebbing. His knees were shaky, his pulse weak. He sat down to read and his vision blurred. The letters on the page turned from green to gold. The lines became waved and jumped over each other, leaving white gaps as if the text had disappeared in some mysterious way. The heat was unbearable, flowing down directly from the tin roof; Dr. Fischelson felt he was inside of an oven. Several times he climbed the four steps to the window and thrust his head out into the cool of the evening breeze. He would remain in that position for so long his knees would become wobbly. "Oh it's a fine breeze," he would murmur, "really delightful," and he would recall that according to Spinoza, morality and happiness were identical, and that the most moral deed a man could perform was to indulge in some pleasure which was not contrary to reason.

II

Dr. Fischelson, standing on the top step at the window and looking out, could see into two worlds. Above him were the heavens, thickly strewn with stars. Dr. Fischelson had never seriously studied astronomy but he could differentiate between the planets, those bodies which like the earth, revolve around the sun, and the fixed stars, themselves distant suns, whose light reaches us a hundred or even a thousand years later. He recognized the constellations which mark the path of the earth in space and that nebulous sash, the Milky Way. Dr. Fischelson owned a small telescope he had bought in Switzerland where he had studied and he particularly enjoyed looking at the moon through it. He could clearly make out on the moon's surface the volcanoes bathed in sunlight and the dark, shadowy craters. He never wearied of gazing at these cracks and crevasses. To him they seemed both near and distant, both substantial and insubstantial. Now and then he would see a shooting star trace a wide arc across the sky and disappear, leaving a fiery trail behind it. Dr. Fischelson would know then that a meteorite had reached our atmosphere, and perhaps some unburned fragment of it had fallen into the ocean or had landed in the desert or perhaps even in some inhabited region. Slowly the stars which had appeared from behind Dr. Fischelson's roof rose until they were shining above the house across the street. Yes, when Dr. Fischelson looked up into the heavens, he became aware of that infinite extension which is, according to Spinoza, one of God's attributes. It comforted Dr. Fischelson to think that although he was only a weak, puny man, a changing mode of the absolutely infinite Substance, he was nevertheless a part of the cosmos, made of the same matter as the celestial bodies; to the extent that he was a part of the Godhead, he knew he could not be destroyed. In such moments, Dr. Fischelson experienced the *Amor Dei Intellectualis* which is, according to the philosopher of Amsterdam, the highest perfection of the mind. Dr. Fischelson breathed deeply, lifted his head as high as his stiff collar permitted and actually felt he was whirling in company with the earth, the sun, the stars of the Milky Way, and the infinite host of galaxies known only to infinite thought. His legs became light and weightless and he grasped the window frame with both hands as if afraid he would lose his footing and fly out into eternity.

When Dr. Fischelson tired of observing the sky, his glance dropped to Market Street below. He could see a long strip extending from Yanash's market to Iron Street with the gas lamps lining it merged into a string of fiery dots. Smoke was issuing from the chimneys on the black, tin roofs; the bakers were heating their ovens, and here and there sparks mingled with the black smoke. The street never looked so noisy and crowded as on a summer evening. Thieves, prostitutes, gamblers, and fences loafed in the square which looked from above like a pretzel covered with poppy seeds. The young men laughed coarsely and the girls shrieked. A peddler with a keg of lemonade on his back pierced the general din with his intermittent cries. A watermelon vendor shouted in a savage voice, and the long knife which he used for cutting the fruit dripped with the blood-like juice. Now and again the street became even more agitated. Fire engines, their heavy wheels clanging, sped by; they were drawn by sturdy black horses which had to be tightly curbed to prevent them from running wild. Next came an ambulance, its siren screaming. Then some thugs had a fight among themselves and the police had to be called. A passerby was robbed and ran about shouting for help. Some wagons loaded with firewood sought to get through into the courtyards where the bakeries were located but the horses could not lift the wheels over the steep curbs and the drivers berated the animals and lashed them with their whips. Sparks rose from the clanging hoofs. It was now long after seven, which was the prescribed closing time for stores, but actually business had only begun. Customers were led in stealthily through back doors. The Russian policemen on the street, having been paid off, noticed nothing of this. Merchants continued to hawk their wares, each seeking to outshout the others.

"Gold, gold, gold," a woman who dealt in rotten oranges shrieked.

"Sugar, sugar, sugar," croaked a dealer of overripe plums.

"Heads, heads, heads," a boy who sold fishheads roared.

Through the window of a *Chassidic* study house across the way, Dr. Fischelson could see boys with long sidelocks swaying over holy volumes, grimacing and studying aloud in singsong voices. Butchers, porters, and fruit dealers were drinking beer in the tavern below. Vapor drifted from the tavern's open door like steam from a bathhouse, and there was the sound of loud music. Outside of the tavern, streetwalkers snatched at drunken soldiers and at workers on their way home from the factories. Some of the men carried bundles of wood on their shoulders, reminding Dr. Fischelson of the wicked who are condemned to kindle their own fires in Hell. Husky record players poured out their raspings through open windows. The liturgy of the high holidays alternated with vulgar vaudeville songs.

Dr. Fischelson peered into the half-lit bedlam and cocked his ears. He knew that the behavior of this rabble was the very antithesis of reason. These people were immersed in the vainest of passions, were drunk with emotions, and, according to Spinoza, emotion was never good. Instead of the pleasure they ran after, all they succeeded in obtaining was disease and prison, shame and the suffering that resulted from ignorance. Even the cats which loitered on the roofs here seemed more savage and passionate than those in other parts of the town. They caterwauled with the voices of women in labor, and like demons scampered up walls and leaped onto eaves and balconies. One of the toms paused at Dr. Fischelson's window and let out a howl which made Dr. Fischelson shudder. The doctor stepped from the window and, picking up a broom, brandished it in front of the black beast's glowing, green eyes. "Scat, begone, you ignorant savage!"—and he rapped the broom handle against the roof until the tom ran off.

III

When Dr. Fischelson had returned to Warsaw from Zurich where he had studied philosophy, a great future had been predicted for him. His friends had known that he was writing an important book on Spinoza. A Jewish Polish journal had invited him to be a contributor; he had been a frequent guest at several wealthy households and he had been made head librarian at the Warsaw synagogue. Although even then he had been considered an old bachelor, the matchmakers had proposed several rich girls for him. But Dr. Fischelson had not taken advantage of these opportunities. He had wanted to be as independent as Spinoza himself. And he had been. But because of his heretical ideas he had come into conflict with the rabbi and had had to resign his post as librarian. For years after that, he had supported himself by giving private lessons in Hebrew and German. Then, when he had become sick, the Berlin Jewish community had voted him a subsidy of five hundred marks a year. This had been made possible through the intervention of the famous Dr. Hildesheimer with whom he corresponded about philosophy. In order to get by on so small a pension, Dr. Fischelson had moved into the attic room and had begun cooking his own meals on a kerosene stove. He had a cupboard which had many drawers, and each drawer was labelled with the food it contained—buckwheat, rice, barley, onions, carrots, potatoes, mushrooms. Once a week Dr. Fischelson put on his widebrimmed black hat, took a basket in one hand and Spinoza's *Ethics* in the other, and went off to the market for his provisions. While he was waiting to be served, he would open the *Ethics*. The merchants knew him and would motion him to their stalls.

"A fine piece of cheese, Doctor—just melts in your mouth."

"Fresh mushrooms, Doctor, straight from the woods."

"Make way for the Doctor, ladies," the butcher would shout. "Please don't block the entrance."

During the early years of his sickness, Dr. Fischelson had still gone in the evening to a café which was frequented by Hebrew teachers and other intellectuals. It had been his habit to sit there and play chess while drinking a half a glass of black coffee. Sometimes he would stop at the bookstores on Holy Cross Street where all sorts of old books and magazines could be purchased cheap. On one occasion a former pupil of his had arranged to meet him at a restaurant one evening. When Dr. Fischelson arrived, he had been surprised to find a group of friends and admirers who forced him to sit at the head of the table while they made speeches about him. But these were things that had happened long ago. Now people were no longer interested in him. He had isolated himself completely and had become a forgotten man. The events of 1905 when the boys of Market Street had begun to organize strikes, throw bombs at police stations, and shoot strike breakers so that the stores were closed even on weekdays had greatly increased his isolation. He began to despise everything associated with the modern Jew—Zionism, socialism, anarchism. The young men in question seemed to him nothing but an ignorant rabble intent on destroying society, society without which no reasonable existence was possible. He still read a Hebrew magazine occasionally, but he felt contempt for modern Hebrew which had no roots in the Bible or the Mishnah. The spelling of Polish words had changed also. Dr. Fischelson concluded that even the so-called spiritual men had abandoned reason and were doing their utmost to pander to the mob. Now and again he still visited a library and browsed through some of the modern histories of philosophy, but he found that the professors did not understand Spinoza, quoted him incorrectly, attributed their own muddled ideas to the philosopher. Although Dr. Fischelson was well aware that anger was an emotion unworthy of those who walk the path of reason, he would become furious, and would quickly close the book and push it from him. "Idiots," he would mutter, "asses, upstarts." And he would vow never again to look at modern philosophy.

IV

Every three months a special mailman who only delivered money orders brought Dr. Fischelson eighty rubles. He expected his quarterly allotment at the beginning of July but as day after day passed and the tall man with the blond moustache and the shiny buttons did not appear, the Doctor grew anxious. He had scarcely a groshen left. Who knows—possibly the Berlin Community had rescinded his subsidy; perhaps Dr. Hildesheimer had died, God forbid; the post office might have made a mistake. Every event has its cause, Dr. Fischelson knew. All was determined, all necessary, and a man of reason had no right to worry. Nevertheless, worry invaded his brain, and buzzed about like the flies. If the worst came to the worst, it occurred to him, he could commit suicide, but then he remembered that Spinoza did not approve of suicide and compared those who took their own lives to the insane.

One day when Dr. Fischelson went out to a store to purchase a composition book, he heard people talking about war. In Serbia somewhere, an Austrian Prince had been shot and the Austrians had delivered an ultimatum to the Serbs. The owner of the store, a young man with a yellow beard and shifty yellow eyes, announced, "We are about to have a small war," and he advised Dr. Fischelson to store up food because in the near future there was likely to be a shortage.

Everything happened so quickly. Dr. Fischelson had not even decided whether it was worthwhile to spend four groshen on a newspaper, and already posters had been hung up announcing mobilization. Men were to be seen walking on the street with round, metal tags on their lapels, a sign that they were being drafted. They were followed by their crying wives. One Monday when Dr. Fischelson descended to the street to buy some food with his last kopecks, he found the stores closed. The owners and their wives stood outside and explained that merchandise was unobtainable. But certain special customers were pulled to one side and let in through back doors. On the street all was confusion. Policemen with swords unsheathed could be seen riding on horseback. A large crowd had gathered around the tavern where, at the command of the Tsar, the tavern's stock of whiskey was being poured into the gutter.

Dr. Fischelson went to his old café. Perhaps he would find some acquaintances there who would advise him. But he did not come across a single person he knew. He decided, then, to visit the rabbi of the synagogue where he had once been librarian, but the sexton with the six-sided skull cap informed him that the rabbi and his family had gone off to the spas. Dr. Fischelson had other old friends in town but he found no one at home. His feet ached from so much walking; black and green spots appeared before his eyes and he felt faint. He stopped and waited for the giddiness to pass. The passers-by jostled him. A dark-eyed high school girl tried to give him a coin. Although the war had just started, soldiers eight abreast were marching in full battle dress—the men were covered with dust and were sunburnt. Canteens were strapped to their sides and they wore rows of bullets across their chests. The bayonets on their rifles gleamed with a cold, green light. They sang with mournful voices. Along with the men came cannons, each pulled by eight horses; their blind muzzles breathed gloomy terror. Dr. Fischelson felt nauseous. His stomach ached; his intestines seemed about to turn themselves inside out. Cold sweat appeared on his face.

"I'm dying," he thought. "This is the end." Nevertheless, he did manage to drag himself home where he lay down on the iron cot and remained, panting and gasping. He must have dozed off because he imagined that he was in his home town, Tishvitz. He had a sore throat and his mother was busy wrapping a stocking stuffed with hot salt around his neck. He could hear talk going on in the house; something about a candle and about how a frog had bitten him. He wanted to go out into the street but they wouldn't let him because a Catholic procession was passing by. Men in long robes, holding double edged axes in their hands, were intoning in Latin as they sprinkled holy water. Crosses gleamed; sacred pictures waved in the air. There was an odor of incense and corpses. Suddenly the sky turned a burning red and the whole world started to burn. Bells were ringing; people rushed madly about. Flocks of birds flew overhead, screeching. Dr. Fischelson awoke with a start. His body was covered with sweat and his throat was now actually sore. He tried to meditate about his extraordinary dream, to find its rational connection with what was happening to him and to comprehend it *sub specie eternitatis*, but none of it made sense. "Alas, the brain is a receptacle for nonsense," Dr. Fischelson thought. "This earth belongs to the mad."

And he once more closed his eyes; once more he dozed; once more he dreamed.

V

The eternal laws, apparently, had not yet ordained Dr. Fischelson's end.

There was a door to the left of Dr. Fischelson's attic room which opened off a dark corridor, cluttered with boxes and baskets, in which the odor of fried onions and laundry soap was always present. Behind this door lived a spinster whom the neighbors called Black Dobbe. Dobbe was tall and lean, and as black as a baker's shovel. She had a broken nose and there was a mustache on her upper lip. She spoke with the hoarse voice of a man and she wore men's shoes. For years Black Dobbe had sold breads, rolls, and bagels which she had bought from the baker at the gate of the house. But one day she and the baker had quarreled and she had moved her business to the market place and now she dealt in what were called "wrinklers" which was a synonym for cracked eggs. Black Dobbe had no luck with men. Twice she had been engaged to baker's apprentices but in both instances they had returned the engagement contract to her. Some time afterwards she had received an engagement contract from an old man, a glazier who claimed that he was divorced, but it had later come to light that he still had a wife. Black Dobbe had a cousin in America, a shoemaker, and repeatedly she boasted that this cousin was sending her passage, but she remained in Warsaw. She was constantly being teased by the women who would say, "There's no hope for you, Dobbe. You're fated to die an old maid." Dobbe always answered, "I don't intend to be a slave for any man. Let them all rot."

That afternoon Dobbe received a letter from America. Generally she would go to Leizer the Tailor and have him read it to her. However, that day Leizer was out and so Dobbe thought of Dr. Fischelson whom the other tenants considered a convert since he never went to prayer. She knocked on the door of the doctor's room but there was no answer. "The heretic is probably out," Dobbe thought but, nevertheless, she knocked once more, and this time the door moved slightly. She pushed her way in and stood there frightened. Dr. Fischelson lay fully clothed on his bed; his face was as yellow as wax; his Adam's apple stuck out prominently; his beard pointed upward. Dobbe screamed; she was certain that he was dead, but—no—his body moved. Dobbe picked up a glass which stood on the table, ran into the corridor, filled the glass with water from the faucet, hurried back, and threw the water into the face of the unconscious man. Dr. Fischelson shook his head and opened his eyes.

"What's wrong with you?" Dobbe asked. "Are you sick?"

"Thank you very much. No."

"Have you a family? I'll call them."

"No family," Dr. Fischelson said.

Dobbe wanted to fetch the barber from across the street but Dr. Fischelson signified that he didn't wish the barber's assistance. Since Dobbe was not going to the market that day, no "wrinklers" being available, she decided to do a good deed. She assisted the sick man to get off the bed and smoothed down the blanket. Then she undressed Dr. Fischelson and prepared some soup for him on the kerosene stove. The sun never entered Dobbe's room, but here squares of sunlight shimmered on the faded walls. The floor was painted red. Over the bed hung a picture of a man who was wearing a broad frill around his neck and had long hair. "Such an old fellow and yet he keeps his place so nice and clean," Dobbe thought approvingly. Dr. Fischelson asked for the *Ethics*, and she gave it to him disapprovingly. She was certain it was a gentile prayer book. Then she began bustling about, brought in a pail of water, swept the floor. Dr. Fischelson ate; after he had finished, he was much stronger and Dobbe asked him to read her the letter.

He read it slowly, the paper trembling in his hands. It came from New York, from Dobbe's cousin. Once more he wrote that he was about to send her a "really important letter" and a ticket to America. By now, Dobbe knew the story by heart and she helped the old man decipher her cousin's scrawl. "He's lying," Dobbe said. "He forgot about me a long time ago." In the evening, Dobbe came again. A candle in a brass holder was burning on the chair next to the bed. Reddish shadows trembled on the walls and ceiling. Dr. Fischelson sat propped up in bed, reading a book. The candle threw a golden light on his forehead which seemed as if cleft in two. A bird had flown in through the window and was perched on the table. For a moment Dobbe was frightened. This man made her think of witches, of black mirrors and corpses wandering around at night and terrifying women. Nevertheless, she took a few steps toward him and inquired, "How are you? Any better?"

"A little, thank you."

"Are you really a convert?" she asked although she wasn't quite sure what the word meant.

"Me, a convert? No, I'm a Jew like any other Jew," Dr. Fischelson answered.

The doctor's assurances made Dobbe feel more at home. She found the bottle of kerosene and lit the stove, and after that she fetched a glass of milk from her room and began cooking kasha. Dr. Fischelson continued to study the *Ethics*, but that evening he could make no sense of the theorems and proofs with their many references to axioms and definitions and other theorems. With trembling hand he raised the book to his eyes and read, "The idea of each modification of the human body does not involve adequate knowledge of the human body itself. . . . The idea of the idea of each modification of the human mind does not involve adequate knowledge of the human mind."

VI

Dr. Fischelson was certain he would die any day now. He made out his will, leaving all of his books and manuscripts to the synagogue library. His clothing and furniture would go to Dobbe since she had taken care of him. But death did not come. Rather his health improved. Dobbe returned to her business in the market, but she visited the old man several times a day, prepared soup for him, left him a glass of tea, and told him news of the war. The Germans had occupied Kalish, Bendin, and Cestechow, and they were marching on Warsaw. People said that on a quiet morning one could hear the rumblings of the cannon. Dobbe reported that the casualties were heavy. "They're falling like flies," she said. "What a terrible misfortune for the women."

She couldn't explain why, but the old man's attic room attracted her. She liked to remove the gold-rimmed books from the bookcase, dust them, and then air them on the window sill. She would climb the few steps to the window and look out through the telescope. She also enjoyed talking to Dr. Fischelson. He told her about Switzerland where he had studied, of the great cities he had passed through, of the high mountains that were covered with snow even in the summer. His father had been a rabbi, he said, and before he, Dr. Fischelson, had become a student, he had attended a yeshiva. She asked him how many languages he knew and it turned out that he could speak and write Hebrew, Russian, German, and French, in addition to Yiddish. He also knew Latin. Dobbe was astonished that such an educated man should live in an attic room on Market Street. But what amazed her most of all was that although he had the title "Doctor," he couldn't write prescriptions. "Why don't you become a real doctor?" she would ask him. "I am a doctor," he would answer. "I'm just not a physician." "What kind of a doctor?" "A doctor of philosophy." Although she had no idea of what this meant, she felt it must be very important. "Oh my blessed mother," she would say, "where did you get such a brain?"

Then one evening after Dobbe had given him his crackers and his glass of tea with milk, he began questioning her about where she came from, who her parents were, and why she had not married. Dobbe was surprised. No one had ever asked her such questions. She told him her story in a quiet voice and stayed until eleven o'clock. Her father had been a porter at the kosher butcher shops. Her mother had plucked chickens in the slaughterhouse. The family had lived in a celler at No. 19 Market Street. When she had been ten, she had become a maid. The man she had worked for had been a fence who bought stolen goods from thieves on the square. Dobbe had

had a brother who had gone into the Russian army and had never returned. Her sister had married a coachman in Praga and had died in childbirth. Dobbe told of the battles between the underworld and the revolutionaries in 1905, of blind Itche and his gang and how they collected protection money from the stores, of the thugs who attacked young boys and girls out on Saturday afternoon strolls if they were not paid money for security. She also spoke of the pimps who drove about in carriages and abducted women to be sold in Buenos Aires. Dobbe swore that some men had even sought to inveigle her into a brothel, but that she had run away. She complained of a thousand evils done to her. She had been robbed; her boy friend had been stolen; a competitor had once poured a pint of kerosene into her basket of bagels; her own cousin, the shoemaker, had cheated her out of a hundred rubles before he had left for America. Dr. Fischelson listened to her attentively. He asked her questions, shook his head, and grunted.

"Well, do you believe in God?" he finally asked her.

"I don't know," she answered. "Do you?"

"Yes, I believe."

"Then why don't you go to synagogue?" she asked.

"God is everywhere," he replied. "In the synagogue. In the marketplace. In this very room. We ourselves are parts of God."

"Don't say such things," Dobbe said. "You frighten me."

She left the room and Dr. Fischelson was certain she had gone to bed. But he wondered why she had not said "good night." "I probably drove her away with my philosophy," he thought. The very next moment he heard her footsteps. She came in carrying a pile of clothing like a peddler.

"I wanted to show you these," she said. "They're my trousseau." And she began to spread out, on the chair, dresses—woolen, silk, velvet. Taking each dress up in turn, she held it to her body. She gave him an account of every item in her trousseau—underwear, shoes, stockings.

"I'm not wasteful, she said. "I'm a saver. I have enough money to go to America."

Then she was silent and her face turned brick-red. She looked at Dr. Fischelson out of the corner of her eyes, timidly, inquisitively. Dr. Fischelson's body suddenly began to shake as if he had the chills. He said, "Very nice, beautiful things." His brow furrowed and he pulled at his beard with two fingers. A sad smile appeared on his toothless mouth and his large fluttering eyes, gazing into the distance through the attic window, also smiled sadly.

VII

The day that Black Dobbe came to the rabbi's chambers and announced that she was to marry Dr. Fischelson, the rabbi's wife thought she had gone mad. But the news had already reached Leizer the Tailor, and had spread to the bakery, as well as to other shops. There were those who thought that the "old maid" was very lucky; the doctor, they said, had a vast hoard of money. But there were others who took the view that he was a run-down degenerate who would give her syphilis. Although Dr. Fischelson had insisted that the wedding be a small, quiet one, a host of guests assembled in the rabbi's rooms. The baker's apprentices who generally went about barefoot, and in their underwear, with paper bags on the tops of their heads, now put on light-colored suits, straw hats, yellow shoes, gaudy ties, and they brought with them huge cakes and pans filled with cookies. They had even managed to find a bottle of vodka although liquor was forbidden in wartime. When the bride and groom entered the rabbi's chamber, a murmur arose from the crowd. The women could not believe their eyes. The woman that they saw was not the one they had known. Dobbe wore a wide-brimmed hat which was amply adorned with cherries, grapes, and plumes, and the dress that she had on was of white silk and was equipped with a train; on her feet were high-heeled shoes, gold in color, and from her thin neck hung a string of imitation pearls. Nor was this all: her fingers sparkled with rings and glittering stones. Her face was veiled. She looked almost like one of those rich brides who were married in the Vienna Hall. The bakers' apprentices whistled mockingly. As for Dr. Fischelson, he was wearing his black coat and broad-toed shoes. He was scarcely able to walk; he was leaning on Dobbe. When he saw the crowd from the doorway, he became frightened and began to retreat, but Dobbe's former employer approached him saying, "Come in, come in, bridegroom. Don't be bashful. We are all brethren now."

The ceremony proceeded according to the law. The rabbi, in a worn satin gabardine, wrote the marriage contract and then had the bride and groom touch his handkerchief as a token of agreement; the rabbi wiped the point of the pen on his skullcap. Several porters who had been called from the street to make up the quorum supported the canopy. Dr. Fischelson put on a white robe as a reminder of the day of his death and Dobbe walked around him seven times as custom required. The light from the braided candles flickered on the walls. The shadows wavered. Having poured wine into a goblet, the rabbi chanted the benedictions in a sad melody. Dobbe uttered only a single cry. As for the other women, they took out their lace handkerchiefs and stood with them in their hands, grimacing. When the baker's boys began to whisper wisecracks to each other, the rabbi put a finger to his lips and murmured, "*Eh nu oh*," as a sign that talking was forbidden. The moment came to slip the wedding ring on the bride's finger, but the bridegroom's hand started to tremble and he had trouble locating Dobbe's index finger. The next thing, according to custom, was the smashing of the glass, but though Dr. Fischelson kicked the goblet several times, it remained unbroken. The girls lowered their heads, pinched each other gleefully, and giggled. Finally one of the apprentices struck the goblet with his heel and it shattered. Even the rabbi could not restrain a smile. After the ceremony the guests drank vodka and ate cookies. Dobbe's former employer came up to Dr. Fischelson and said, "*Mazel tov*, bridegroom. Your luck should be as good as your wife." "Thank you, thank you," Dr. Fischelson murmured, "but I don't look forward to any luck." He was anxious to return as quickly as possible to his attic room. He felt a pressure in his stomach and his chest ached. His face had become greenish. Dobbe had suddenly become angry. She pulled back her veil and called out to the crowd, "What are you laughing at? This isn't a show." And without picking up the cushion-cover in which the gifts were wrapped, she returned with her husband to their rooms on the fifth floor.

Dr. Fischelson lay down on the freshly made bed in his room and began reading the *Ethics*. Dobbe had gone back to her own room. The doctor had explained to her that he was an old man, that he was sick and without strength. He had promised her nothing. Nevertheless she returned wearing a silk nightgown, slippers with pompoms, and with her hair hanging down over her shoulders. There was a smile on her face, and she was bashful and hesitant. Dr. Fischelson trembled and the *Ethics* dropped from his hands. The candle went out. Dobbe groped for Dr. Fischelson in the dark and kissed his mouth. "My dear husband," she whispered to him, "*Mazel tov*."

What happened that night could be called a miracle. If Dr.

Fischelson hadn't been convinced that every occurrence is in accordance with the laws of nature, he would have thought that Black Dobbe had bewitched him. Powers long dormant awakened in him. Although he had had only a sip of the benediction wine, he was as if intoxicated. He kissed Dobbe and spoke to her of love. Long forgotten quotations from Klopfstock, Lessing, Goethe, rose to his lips. The pressures and aches stopped. He embraced Dobbe, pressed her to himself, was again a man as in his youth. Dobbe was faint with delight; crying, she murmured things to him in a Warsaw slang which he did not understand. Later, Dr. Fischelson slipped off into the deep sleep young men know. He dreamed that he was in Switzerland and that he was climbing mountains—running, falling, flying. At dawn he opened his eyes; it seemed to him that someone had blown into his ears. Dobbe was snoring. Dr. Fischelson quietly got out of bed. In his long nightshirt he approached the window, walked up the steps and looked out in wonder. Market Street was asleep, breathing with a deep stillness. The gas lamps were flickering. The black shutters on the stores were fastened with iron bars. A cool breeze was blowing. Dr. Fischelson looked up at the sky. The black arch was thickly sown with stars—there were green, red, yellow, blue stars; there were large ones and small ones, winking and steady ones. There were those that were clustered in dense groups and those that were alone. In the higher sphere, apparently, little notice was taken of the fact that a certain Dr. Fischelson had in his declining days married someone called Black Dobbe. Seen from above even the Great War was nothing but a temporary play of the modes. The myriads of fixed stars continued to travel their destined courses in unbounded space. The comets, planets, satellites, asteroids kept circling these shining centers. Worlds were born and died in cosmic upheavals. In the chaos of nebulae, primeval matter was being formed. Now and again a star tore loose, and swept across the sky, leaving behind it a fiery streak. It was the month of August when there are showers of meteors. Yes, the divine substance was extended and had neither beginning nor end; it was absolute, indivisible, eternal, without duration, infinite in its attributes. Its waves and bubbles danced in the universal cauldron, seething with change, following the unbroken chain of causes and effects, and he, Dr. Fischelson, with his unavoidable fate, was part of this. The doctor closed his eyelids and allowed the breeze to cool the sweat on his forehead and stir the hair of his beard. He breathed deeply of the midnight air, supported his shaky hands on the window sill and murmured, "Divine Spinoza, forgive me. I have become a fool."

Translated by
Martha Glicklich and
Cecil Hemley

The Black Wedding

I

Aaron Naphtali, Rabbi of Tzivkev, had lost three-fourths of his followers. There was talk in the rabbinical courts that Rabbi Aaron Naphtali alone had been responsible for driving away his Chassidim. A rabbinical court must be vigilant, more adherents must be acquired. One has to find devices so that the following will not diminish. But Rabbi Aaron Naphtali was apathetic. The study house was old and toadstools grew unmolested on the walls. The ritual bath fell to ruin. The beadles were tottering old men, deaf and half-blind. The rabbi passed his time practicing miracle-working cabala.

It was said that Rabbi Aaron Naphtali wanted to imitate the feats of the ancient ones, to tap wine from the wall and create pigeons through combinations of holy names. It was even said that he molded a golem secretly in his attic. Moreover, Rabbi Naphtali had no son to succeed him, only one daughter named Hindele. Who would be eager to follow a rabbi under these circumstances? His enemies contended that Rabbi Aaron Naphtali was sunk in melancholy, as were his wife and Hindele. The latter, at fifteen, was already reading esoteric books and periodically went into seclusion like the holy men. It was rumored that Hindele wore a fringed garment underneath her dress like that worn by her saintly grandmother after whom she had been named.

Rabbi Aaron Naphtali had strange habits. He shut himself in his chamber for days and would not come out to welcome visitors. When he prayed, he put on two pairs of phylacteries at once. On Friday afternoons, he read the prescribed section of the Pentateuch—not from a book but from the parchment scroll itself. The rabbi had learned to form letters with the penmanship of the ancient scribes, and he used this script for writing amulets. A little bag containing one of these amulets hung from the neck of each of his followers. It was known that the rabbi warred constantly with the evil ones. His grandfather, the old Rabbi of Tzivkev, had exorcised a dybbuk from a young girl and the evil spirits had revenged themselves upon the grandson. They had not been able to bring harm to the old man because he had been blessed by the Saint of Kozhenitz. His son, Rabbi Hirsch, Rabbi Aaron Naphtali's father, died young. The grandson, Rabbi Aaron Naphtali, had to contend with the vengeful devils all his life. He lit a candle, they extinguished it. He placed a volume on the bookshelf, they knocked it off. When he undressed in the ritual bath, they hid his silk coat and his fringed garment.

Often, sounds of laughter and wailing seemed to come from the rabbi's chimney. There was a rustling behind the stove. Steps were heard on the roof. Doors opened by themselves. The stairs would screech although nobody had stepped on them. Once the rabbi laid his pen on the table and it sailed out through the open window as if carried by an unseen hand. The rabbi's hair turned white at forty. His back was bent, his hands and feet trembled like those of an ancient man. Hindele often suffered attacks of yawning; red flushes spread over her face, her throat ached, there was a buzzing in her ears. At such times incantations had to be made to drive away the evil eye.

The rabbi used to say, "They will not leave me in peace, not even for a moment." And he stamped his foot and asked the beadle to give him his grandfather's cane. He rapped it against each corner of the room and cried out, "You will not work your evil tricks on me!"

But the black hosts gained ascendency just the same. One autumn day the rabbi became ill with erysipelas and it was soon apparent that he would not recover from his sickness. A doctor was sent for from a nearby town, but on the way the axle of his coach broke and he could not complete the journey. A second physician was called for, but a wheel of his carriage came loose and rolled into a ditch, and the horse sprained his leg. The rabbi's wife went to the memorial chapel of her husband's deceased grandfather to pray, but the vindictive demons tore her bonnet from her head. The rabbi lay in bed with a swollen face and a shrunken beard, and for two days he did not speak a word. Quite suddenly he opened an eye and cried out, "They have won!"

Hindele, who would not leave her father's bed, wrung her hands and began to wail in despair, "Father, what's to become of me?"

The rabbi's beard trembled. "You must keep silent if you are to be spared."

There was a great funeral. Rabbis had come from half of Poland. The women predicted that the rabbi's widow would not last much longer. She was white as a corpse. She hadn't enough strength in her feet to follow the hearse and two women had to support her. At the burial she tried to throw herself into the grave and they could barely restrain her. All through the Seven Days of Mourning, she ate nothing. They tried to force a spoon of chicken broth into her mouth, but she was unable to swallow it. When the Thirty Days of Mourning had passed, the rabbi's wife still had not left her bed. Physicians were brought to her but to no avail. She herself foresaw the day of her death and she foretold it to the minute. After her funeral, the rabbi's disciples began to look around for a young man for Hindele. They had tried to find a match for her even before her father's death, but her father had been difficult to please. The son-in-law would eventually have to take the rabbi's place and who was worthy to sit in the Tzivkev rabbinical chair? Whenever the rabbi finally gave his approval, his wife found fault with the young man. Besides, Hindele was known to be sick, to keep too many fast days and to fall into a swoon when things did not go her way. Nor was she attractive. She was short, frail, had a large head, a skinny neck, and flat breasts. Her hair was bushy. There was an insane look in her black eyes. However, since Hindele's dowry was a following of thousands of Chassidim, a candidate was found, Reb Simon, son of the Yampol Rabbi. His older brother having died, Reb Simon would become Rabbi of Yampol after his father's death. Yampol and Tzivkev had much in common. If they were to unite, the glory of former times would return. True, Reb Simon was a divorced man with five children. But as Hindele was an orphan, who would protest? The Tzivkev Chassidim had one stipulation—that after his father's death, Reb Simon should reside in Tzivkev.

Both Tzivkev and Yampol were anxious to bring the union about. Immediately after the marriage contract was written, wedding preparations were begun, because the Tzivkev rabbinical chair had to be filled. Hindele had not yet seen her husband-to-be. She was told that he was a widower, and nothing was said about the five children. The wedding was a noisy one. Chassidim came from all parts of Poland. The followers of the Yampol court and those of the Tzivkev court began to address one another by the familiar "thou." The inns were full. The innkeeper brought straw mattresses down from the attic and put them out in corridors, granaries, and tool sheds, to accommodate the large crowd. Those who opposed the match foretold that Yampol would engulf Tzivkev. The Chassidim of Yampol were known for their crudeness. When they played, they became boisterous. They drank long draughts of brandy from tin mugs and became drunk. When they danced, the floors heaved under them. When an adversary of Yampol spoke harshly of their rabbi, he was beaten. There was a custom in Yampol that when the wife of a young man gave birth to a girl, the father was placed on a table and lashed thirty-nine times with a strap.

Old women came to Hindele to warn her that it would not be easy to be a daughter-in-law in the Yampol court. Her future mother-in-law, an old woman, was known for her wickedness. Reb Simon and his younger brothers had wild ways. The mother had chosen large women for her sons and the frail Hindele would not please her. Reb Simon's mother had consented to the match only because of Yampol's ambitions regarding Tzivkev.

From the time that the marriage negotiations started until the wedding, Hindele did not stop crying. She cried at the celebration of the writing of the marriage contract, she cried when the tailors fitted her trousseau, she cried when she was led to the ritual bath. There she was ashamed to undress for the immersion before the attendants and the other women, and they had to tear off her stays and her underpants. She would not let them remove from her neck the little bag which contained an amber charm and the tooth of a wolf. She was afraid to immerse herself in the water. The two attendants who led her into the bath, held her tightly by her wrists and she trembled like the sacrificial chicken the day before Yom Kippur. When Reb Simon lifted the veil from Hindele's face after the wedding, she saw him for the first time. He was a tall man with a broad fur hat, a pitch-black disheveled beard, wild eyes, a broad nose, thick lips, and a long moustache. He gazed at her like an animal. He breathed noisily and smelled of perspiration. Clusters of hair grew out of his nostrils and ears. His hands, too, had a growth of hair as thick as fur. The moment Hindele saw him she knew what she had suspected long before —that her bridegroom was a demon and that the wedding was nothing but black magic, a satanic hoax. She wanted to call out "Hear, O Israel" but she remembered her father's deathbed admonition to keep silent. How strange that the moment Hindele understood that her husband was an evil spirit, she could immediately discern what was true and what was false. Although she saw herself sitting in her mother's living room, she knew she was really in a forest. It appeared to be light, but she knew it was dark. She was surrounded by Chassidim with fur hats and satin gabardines, as well as by women who wore silk bonnets and velvet capes, but she knew it was all imaginary and that the fancy garments hid heads grown with elf-locks, goose-feet, unhuman navels, long snouts. The sashes of the young men were snakes in reality, their sable hats were actually hedgehogs, their beards clusters of worms. The men spoke Yiddish and sang familiar songs, but the noise they made was really the bellowing of oxen, the hissing of vipers, the howling of wolves. The musicians had tails, and horns grew from their heads. The maids who attended Hindele had canine paws, hoofs of calves, snouts of pigs. The wedding jester was all beard and tongue. The so-called relatives on the groom's side were lions, bears, boars. It was raining in the forest and a wind was blowing. It thundered and flashed lightning. Alas, this was not a human wedding, but a Black Wedding. Hindele knew, from reading holy books, that demons sometimes married human virgins whom they later carried away behind the black mountains to cohabit with them and sire their children. There was only one thing to do in such a case—not to comply with them, never willingly submit to them, to let them get everything by force as one kind word spoken to Satan is equivalent to sacrificing to the idols. Hindele remembered the story of Joseph De La Rinah and the misfortune that befell him when he felt sorry for the evil one and gave him a pinch of tobacco.

II

Hindele did not want to march to the wedding canopy, and she planted her feet stubbornly on the floor, but the bridesmaids dragged her. They half-pulled her, half-carried her. Imps in the images of girls held the candles and formed an aisle for her. The canopy was a braid of reptiles. The rabbi who performed the ceremony was under contract to Samael. Hindele submitted to nothing. She refused to hold out her finger for the ring and had to be forced to do so. She would not drink from the goblet and they poured some wine into her mouth. Hobgoblins performed all the wedding rites. The evil spirit who appeared in the likeness of Reb Simon was wearing a white robe. He stepped on the bride's foot with his hoof so that he might rule over her. Then he smashed the wine glass. After the ceremony, a witch danced toward the bride carrying a braided bread. Presently the bride and groom were served the so-called soup, but Hindele spat everything into her handkerchief. The musicians played a Kossack, an Angry Dance, a Scissors Dance and a Water Dance. But their webbed roosters' feet peeped out from under their robes. The wedding hall was nothing but a forest swamp, full of frogs, mooncalves, monsters, each with his ticks and grimaces. The Chassidim presented the couple with assorted gifts, but these were devices to ensnare Hindele in the net of evil. The wedding jester recited sad poems and funny poems, but his voice was that of a parrot.

They called Hindele to dance the Good-Luck dance, but she did not want to get up, knowing it was actually a Bad-Luck dance. They urged her, pushed her, pinched her. Little imps stuck pins into her thighs. In the middle of the dance, two she-demons grabbed her by the arms and carried her away into a bedroom which was actually a dark cave full of thistles, scavengers, and rubbish. While these females whispered to her the duties of a bride, they spat in her ear. Then she was thrown upon a heap of mud which was supposed to be linen. For a long while, Hindele lay in that cave, surrounded by darkness, poison weeds and lice. So great was her anxiety that she couldn't even pray. Then the devil to whom she was espoused entered. He assailed her with cruelty, tore off her clothes, martyred her, abused her, shamed her. She wanted to scream for help but she restrained herself knowing that if she uttered a sound she would be lost forever.

All night long Hindele felt herself lying in blood and pus. The one who had raped her snored, coughed, hissed like an adder. Before dawn a group of hags ran into the room, pulled the sheet from under her, inspected it, sniffed it, began to dance. That night never ended. True, the sun rose. It was not really the sun, though, but a bloody sphere which somebody hung in the sky. Women came to coax the bride with smooth talk and cunning but Hindele did not pay any attention to their babble. They spat at her, flattered her, said incantations, but she did not answer them. Later a doctor was brought to her, but Hindele saw that he was a horned buck. No, the black powers could not rule her, and Hindele kept on spiting them. Whatever they bade her do, she did the opposite. She threw the soup and marchpane into the slop can. She dumped the chickens and squab which they baked for her into the outhouse. She found a page of a psalter in the mossy forest and she recited psalms furtively. She also remembered a few passages of the Torah and of the prophets. She acquired more and more courage to pray to God-Almighty to save her. She mentioned the names of holy angels as well those of her illustrious ancestors like the Baal Shem, Rabbi Leib Sarah's, Rabbi Pinchos Korzer and the like.

Strange, that although she was only one and the others were multitudes, they could not overcome her. The one who was disguised as her husband tried to bribe her with sweet-talk and gifts, but she did not satisfy him. He came to her but she turned away from him. He kissed her with his wet lips and petted her with clammy fingers, but she did not let him have her. He forced himself on her, but she tore at his beard, pulled at his sidelocks, scratched his forehead. He ran away from her bloody. It became clear to Hindele that her power was not of this world. Her father was interceding for her. He came to her in his shroud and comforted her. Her mother revealed herself to her and gave her advice. True, the earth was full of evil spirits, but up above angels were hovering. Sometimes Hindele heard the angel Gabriel fighting and fencing with

Satan. Bevies of black dogs and crows came to help him, but the saints drove them away with their palm leaves and hosannahs. The barking and the crowing were drowned out by the song which Hindele's grandfather used to sing Saturday evenings and which was called "The Sons of the Mansion."

But horror of horrors, Hindele became pregnant. A devil grew inside her. She could see him through her own belly as through a cobweb: half-frog, half-ape, with eyes of a calf and scales of a fish. He ate her flesh, sucked her blood, scratched her with his claws, bit her with his pointed teeth. He was already chattering, calling her mother, cursing with vile language. She had to get rid of him, stop his gnawing at her liver. Nor was she able to bear his blasphemy and mockery. Besides, he urinated in her and defiled her with his excrement. Miscarriage was the only way out, but how bring it on? Hindele struck her stomach with her fist. She jumped, threw herself down, crawled, all to get rid of that devil's bastard, but to no avail. He grew quickly and showed inhuman strength, pushed and tore at her insides. His skull was of copper, his mouth of iron. He had capricious urges. He told her to eat lime from the wall, the shell of an egg, all kinds of garbage. And if she refused, he squeezed her gall bladder. He stank like a skunk and Hindele fainted from the stench. In her swoon, a giant appeared to her with one eye in his forehead. He talked to her from a hollowed tree saying, "Give yourself up, Hindele, you are one of us."

"No, never."

"We will take revenge."

He flogged her with a fiery rod and yelled abuses. Her head became as heavy as a millstone from fear. The fingers of her hands became big and hard like rolling pins. Her mouth puckered as from eating unripe fruit. Her ears felt as if they were full of water. Hindele was not free any more. The hosts rolled her in muck, mire, slime. They immersed her in baths of pitch. They flayed her skin. They pulled the nipples of her breasts with pliers. They tortured her ceaselessly but she remained mute. Since the males could not persuade her, the female devils attacked her. They laughed with abandon, they braided their hair around her, choked her, tickled her, and pinched her. One giggled, another cried, another wiggled like a whore. Hindele's belly was big and hard as a drum and Belial sat in her womb. He pushed with elbows and pressed with his skull. Hindele lay in labor. One she-devil was a mid-wife and the other an aide. They had hung all kinds of charms over her canopied bed and they put a knife and a Book of Creation under her pillow, the way the evil ones imitate the humans in all manners. Hindele was in her birth throes, but she remembered that she was not allowed to groan. One sigh and she would be lost. She must restrain herself in the name of her holy forbears.

Suddenly the black one inside her pushed with all his might. A piercing scream tore itself from Hindele's throat and she was swallowed in darkness. Bells were ringing as on a gentile holiday. A hellish fire flared up. It was as red as blood, as scarlet as leprosy. The earth opened like in the time of Korah, and Hindele's canopied bed began to sink into the abyss. Hindele had lost everything, this world and the world to come. In the distance she heard the crying of women, the clapping of hands, blessings and good wishes, while she flew straight into the castle of Asmodeus where Lilith, Namah, Machlath, Hurmizah rule.

In Tzivkev and in the neighborhood the tidings spread that Hindele had given birth to a male child by Reb Simon of Yampol. The mother had died in childbirth.

Translated by Martha Glicklich

A Tale of Two Liars

I

A lie can only thrive on truth; lies, heaped one upon another, lack substance. Let me tell you how I manipulated two liars by pulling the strings, making them dance to my tune.

The woman of the pair, Glicka Genendel, arrived in Janov several weeks before Passover, claiming to be the widow of the Zosmir rabbi; she was childless, she said, and anxious to remarry. She was not required to participate first in the levirate marriage ceremony, she explained, since her husband had been an only son. She was settling in Janov because a soothsayer had prophesied that she would meet a mate in this town. She boasted that her late husband had studied the Talmud with her, and, to prove it, she sprinkled her conversation with quotations. She was a source of constant wonder to the townspeople. True, she was no beauty. Her nose sloped like a ram's horn, but she did have a pleasantly pale complexion, and large, dark eyes; in addition, her chin was pointed and her tongue glib. There was a bounce to her walk, and she scattered witticisms wherever she went.

No matter what occurred, she could remember a similar experience; for every sorrow, she offered comfort, for every illness, a remedy. She was dazzling in her high-buttoned shoes, woolen dress, fringed silk shawl, and head-band festooned with precious gems. There was slush on the ground, and so she skipped nimbly from stone to stone and plank to plank, holding her skirt daintily in one hand, and her satchel in the other. She brought joy wherever she went, although she did solicit donations, but the donations were not for herself, God forbid. What she got, she turned over to poor brides and indigent mothers-to-be. Because she was such a doer of good deeds, she boarded at the inn free of charge. The guests enjoyed her quips and yarns, and, you may be sure, the innkeeper lost nothing by the arrangement.

She was immediately showered with proposals, and she accepted them all. In almost no time, the town's widowers and divorcees were at each other's throats, each determined to have this remarkable "catch" for himself. Meanwhile, she ran up bills for dresses and underclothing, and dined well on roast squab and egg-noodles. She was also active in community affairs, helping in the preparation of the mill for Passover, examining the sheaves of Pashcal wheat, assisting in the baking of the matzoths, joking with the bakers as they kneaded, rolled, perforated, poured, and cut. She even went to the rabbi so that the ceremony of selling the leavened bread which she had left behind in Zosmir could be performed. The rabbi's wife invited Glicka Genendel to the Seder. She came adorned in a white satin gown and heavy with jewelry, and chanted the Haggadah as fluently as any man. Her coquetry made the rabbi's daughters and daughters-in-law jealous. The widows and divorcees of Janov were simply consumed with rage. It seemed as if this crafty woman would snare for herself the wealthiest widower in town, and, without as much as a by-your-leave, become the richest matron in Janov. But it was I, the Arch-Devil, who saw to it that she was supplied with a mate.

He showed up in Janov during Passover, arriving in an ornate *britska* which had been hired for the occasion. His story was that he had come from Palestine to solicit charity, and he, like Glicka, had also recently lost his spouse. His trunk was banded with brass; he smoked a hookah, and the bag in which he carried his prayer shawl was made of leather. He put on two sets of phylacteries when he prayed, and his conversation was sprinkled with Aramaic. His name was Reb Yomtov, he said. He was a tall, thin man, with a pointed beard, and though he dressed like any other townsman in caftan, fur cap, breeches, and high hose, his swarthy face and burning eyes brought to mind a Sephardic Jew from Yemen or Persia. He insisted that he had seen with his own eyes Noah's Ark on Mount Ararat, and that the splinters he sold at six farthings a piece had been carved from one of its planks. He also had in his possession coins over which Yehudah the Chassid had cast a spell, along with a sack of chalky earth from Rachel's grave. This sack, apparently, had no bottom as it never grew empty.

He too put up at the inn, and soon he and Glicka Genendel were friends, to their mutual delight. When they traced back their ancestry, they discovered that they were distant relatives, both descended from some saint or other. They would chat with each other and plot deep into the night. Glicka Genendel hinted that she found Reb Yomtov attractive. She didn't have to spell it out for him—they understood each other.

Those two were in a hurry. That is—I, Sammael, spurred them on. So the Articles of Engagement were drawn up, and after the prospective bride had signed, her husband-to-be gave as his gifts an engagement ring and a necklace of pearls. He had received them, he said, from his first wife who had been an heiress in Baghdad. In return, Glicka Genendel presented to her betrothed a sapphire-studded cover for the Sabbath loaf which she had inherited from her late father, the famous philanthropist.

Then, just at the end of Passover, there was a great to-do in town. One of the very substantial citizens, a Reb Kathriel Abba, complained to the rabbi that Glicka Genendel was engaged to him and that he had given her thirty gulden for a trousseau.

The widow was enraged at these allegations.

"It's just spite," she said, "because I wouldn't sin with him."

She demanded that her slanderer pay her thirty gulden as restitution. But Reb Kathriel Abba stood by the truth of his accusation, and offered to take an oath before the Holy Scroll. Glicka Genendel was just as determined to defend her statement in front of the Black Candles. However an epidemic was raging in the town at the time and the women were fearful that all this oath-taking would end up costing them the lives of their children, and so the rabbi finally ruled that Glicka was obviously a good woman and he commanded that Reb Kathriel Abba apologize and pay the settlement.

Immediately after that, a beggar arrived from Zosmir and surprised everyone by explaining that the late rabbi's wife could not be visiting in Janov, since she was in Zosmir, God be praised, with her husband who was not the least bit dead. There was great excitement and the townspeople rushed to the inn to punish the fraudulent widow for her infamous lie. She was not at all upset and merely explained that she had said "Kosmir," not "Zosmir." Once more all was well, and the preparations for the wedding continued. The wedding had been set for the thirty-third day of the Feast of Omer.

But there was one additional incident before the wedding. For one reason or another, Glicka Genendel thought it wise to consult a goldsmith about the pearls which Reb Yomtov had given her. The jeweler weighed and examined the pearls and declared them to be paste. The wedding was off, Glicka Genendel announced, and informed the bridegroom to that effect. He speedily rose to his own defense; in the first place, the jeweler was incompetent; there couldn't be any doubt of that since he, Reb Yomtov, had personally paid ninety-five drachmas for the pearls in Stamboul; in the second place, immediately after the ceremony, God willing, he would replace the counterfeits with the genuine article, and finally he wanted to point out, just in passing, that the cover Glicka Genendel had given him was not embroidered with sapphires, but with beads, and beads, mind you, that sold for three groshen a dozen in the market. Therefore the two liars were quits, and with their differences patched up, stood under the marriage canopy together.

However, later that night, the delegate from the Holy Land discovered that he had not married a spring chicken. She took off her wig, releasing a mass of gray hair. A hag stood before him, and he ransacked his brain to find a solution. But since he was a professional he didn't show his irritation. Nevertheless, Glicka Genendel was taking no chances; to make sure of her husband's love, she fashioned a love charm. She plucked hair from a private place and wove it around a button of her dear one's dressing gown; in addition, she washed her breasts in water which she then poured into a potion for him to drink. As she went about performing this significant business, she sang:

As a tree has its shadow,
Let me have my love.
As wax melts in a fire,
Let him burn to my touch.
Now and forever,
In me be his trust,
Trapped in desire
Until all turn to dust.
Amen. Selah.

11

"Is there any reason why we should stay in Janov?" Reb Yomtov asked when the seven days of nuptial benediction were over. "I would prefer to return to Jerusalem. After all we have a fine house waiting for us near the Wailing Wall. But first I must visit a few towns in Poland to make collections. There are my yeshiva students to think of and then also funds are required to erect a prayer house on the grave of Reb Simon Bar Johai. The last is a very expensive project and will require a good deal of money."

"What towns will you visit? And how long will you be away?" Glicka Genendel asked.

"I intend to stop off at Lemberg, Brod, and some of the other towns in their immediate vicinity. I should be back by midsummer, God willing. We should be in Jerusalem in time to celebrate the High Holy days."

"That's fine," she said. "I'll use the time to visit the graves of my dear ones and to say goodbye to my relatives in Kalish. God speed, and don't forget the way home."

They embraced warmly, and she presented him with some preserves and cookies, and a jar of chicken fat. She also gave him an amulet to protect him from highwaymen, and he set off on his journey.

When he arrived at the River San he halted, turned his carriage around, and drove off on the Lublin road. His destination was Piask, a small town on the outskirts of Lublin. The inhabitants of Piask had a fine reputation. It was said that you did not put on a prayer shawl there, if you didn't want your phylacteries stolen; the point being that in Piask you dared not cover your eyes even that long. Well, it was in that splendid place that the legate sought out the assistant rabbi and had the scribe write out a Bill of Divorcement for Glicka Genendel. He then sent the papers by messenger to Janov. The whole thing cost Reb Yomtov five gulden, but he considered it money well spent.

This done, Reb Yomtov rode into Lublin and preached at the famous Marshall Synagogue. He had a tongue of silver, and chose a Lithuanian accent for his sermon. Beyond the Cossack Steppes and the land of the Tartars, he explained, dwelt the last of the Chazars. This ancient people were cave-dwellers, fought with bow and arrow, sacrificed in the Biblical manner, and spoke Hebrew. He had in his possession a letter from their chieftain, Yedidi Ben Achitov, a grandson of the Chazar king, and he exhibited a parchment scroll which bore the name of many witnesses. These distant Jews who were waging such a stubborn war against the enemies of Israel and who were the only ones who knew the secret road to the river Sambation, were in dire need of funds, he pointed out, and he went through the crowd collecting money for them.

As he circulated among the people, he was approached by a blond-haired young man who asked him his name.

"Solomon Simeon," Reb Yomtov replied, merely lying out of habit.

The young man wished to know where he was staying, and when he heard that it was at the inn, he shook his head.

"Such a needless expense," he said. "And why associate with riff-raff? I have a large house, God be praised. In it there is a guest room and holy books to spare. I am at business all day, and I have no children (may you be spared my fate), so you won't be disturbed. My wife would be honored to have a scholar in the house, and my mother-in-law, who is visiting us, is a learned woman, and a matchmaker in the bargain. Should you need a wife, she will find you one, and a real catch, I can assure you."

"Alas, I am a widower," the spurious Reb Solomon Simeon said, putting on a glum expression, "but I cannot think of marriage at this time. My dear wife was a true grandchild of Rabbi Sabbatai Kohen, and though she is gone three years now, I cannot forget her." And Reb Yomtov continued to sigh mournfully.

"Who are we to question the wisdom of the Almighty?" the young man asked. "It is written in the Talmud that one must not grieve too long."

On their way to the young man's house, the two carried on a lively discussion concerning the Torah, with occasional digressions to more worldly matters. The young man was amazed at his guest's knowledge and intellect.

As he mounted the steps of the young man's house, Reb Yomtov was almost overcome by the odors he smelled. His mouth watered. Fowl was being roasted, cabbage boiled. "Praised be His name," he thought to himself, "Lublin looks like it will be very satisfactory. If his wife wants a learned man, she will certainly have one. And who can tell, I may be strong enough to produce a miracle, and they may yet have a son and heir. Nor if a rich bride becomes available, will I turn her down either."

The door swung open, admitting Reb Yomtov to a kitchen whose walls were covered with copper pans. An oil lamp hung from the ceiling. In the room were two women, the lady of the house and a servant girl; they stood at the stove in which a goose was being roasted. The young man introduced his guest (it was obvious that he was proud to have brought home such a man) and his wife smiled warmly at Reb Yomtov.

"My husband does not praise everyone so highly," she said. "You must be a very unusual man. It is good to have you here. My mother is in the dining room, and will make you welcome. Should you want anything, don't hesitate to let her know."

Reb Yomtov thanked his hostess, and walked in the direction she had indicated, but his host lingered for a moment in the kitchen, no doubt anxious to amplify further on what a distinguished visitor they were entertaining.

Piously Reb Yomtov kissed the *mezuzah*, and opened the door to the adjoining room. What lay beyond was even better than what had gone before. The room which he was entering was most elegantly furnished. But then he stopped. What was this he saw? His heart dropped, and words failed him. No, it couldn't be; he was dreaming. He was seeing a mirage. No, it was witchcraft. For there stood his former bride, his Janov sweetheart. There could be no doubt about it. This was Glicka Genendel.

"Yes, it is me," she said, and once more he heard that familiar shrewish voice."

"What are you doing here?" he asked. "You said you were going to Kalish."

"I have come to visit my daughter."

"Your daughter? You told me you had no children."

"I thought you were on your way to Lemberg," she said.

"Didn't you get the divorce papers?"

"What divorce papers?"

"Those I sent by messenger."

"I tell you I've received nothing. May all my bad dreams be visited on your head."

Reb Yomtov saw how things were: he had fallen into a trap; there was no means of escape. His host would enter at any moment, and he would be exposed.

"I have been guilty of a great foolishness," he said, summoning up all of his courage. "These people are under the impression that I am a traveler just returned from the land of the Chazars. It's to your interest to protect me. You don't want to have me driven out of town and remain a deserted wife forever. Don't say anything, and I swear by my beard and earlocks that I'll make it worthwhile for you."

Glicka Genendel had a good many abusive things that she was longing to say, but just then her son-in-law entered. He was beaming.

"We have a most distinguished guest in the house," he said. "This is Reb Solomon Simeon of Lithuania. He has just returned from a visit to the Chazars, who, as you know, live very close to the Lost Ten Tribes." And to Reb Yomtov he explained, "My mother-in-law is to depart shortly for the Holy Land. She is married to a Reb Yomtov, a delegate from Jerusalem and a descendant of the house of David. Possibly you've heard of him?"

"I most certainly have," Reb Yomtov said.

By this time, Glicka Genendel had recovered her composure sufficiently to say, "Do be seated, Reb Solomon Simeon, and tell us all about the Lost Ten Tribes. Did you actually see the River Sambation hurling stones? Were you able to cross over safely and meet the king?"

But the moment her son-in-law left the room, she was on her feet hissing, "Well, what about it, Reb Solomon Simeon? Where is my payment?"

Before he had a chance to say anything, she grabbed him by his lapels and thrust her hand into the inside pocket of his coat. There she found a pouch of ducats, and it took only a very few seconds for her to transfer them to her stocking. For good measure, she pulled a handful of hair from his beard.

"I'm going to teach you a lesson," she said. "Don't think that you're going to get away from here in one piece. Your descendants to the tenth generation will beware of being such an outrageous liar." And she spat in his face. He took out his handkerchief and wiped himself off. Then the lady of the house and the servant girl came in and set the table for supper. In honor of the visitor, the host descended to the wine cellar to fetch a bottle of dry wine.

III

After supper, Glicka Genendel made up a bed for the guest.

"Now get in there," she said, "and I don't want you to do so much as stir a whisker. After the others are asleep, I'll be back for a little chat."

And to prevent him from escaping she impounded his overcoat, cap, and shoes. Reb Yomtov said his prayers and went to bed. He lay there trying to think of some way out of his predicament; and it was at this point that I, the Evil One, materialized.

"Why hang around here like a trussed calf awaiting the slaughterer?" I said. "Open the window and run."

"Just how am I to manage that," he asked, "with no clothes or shoes?"

"It's warm enough outside," I told him. "You're not going to get sick. Just find your way to Piask, and once there, you'll make out all right. Anything is better than remaining with this termagant."

As usual he heeded my counsel. He rose from the bed, threw open the window, and began the descent. I saw to it, however, that there was an obstacle in his path, and he lost his footing and fell, spraining his ankle. For a moment he lay on the ground unconscious. But I revived him.

He forced himself to his feet. It was a very dark night. Barefoot, half-naked, limping, he started off down the Piask road.

While this was going on, Glicka Genendel was occupied otherwise. She could hear the snores of her daughter and son-in-law coming from their bedroom, and so she got up, put on her wrapper, and tiptoed to the chamber of her best beloved. To her astonishment she saw that the bed was unoccupied and the window open. Before she could scream, however, I appeared to her.

"Now what's the sense of that?" I asked her. "It's not a crime for a man to get out of bed, is it? He hasn't stolen anything. The fact is it's you who've done the stealing, and if he's caught, he'll tell about the money you took from him. You're the one who'll suffer."

"Well, what shall I do?" she asked me.

"Don't you see? Steal your daughter's jewel box; then begin to yell. If he's apprehended he'll be the one who's thrown in jail. That way your revenge is certain."

The idea appealed to her and she took my advice. A few shrieks and she had awakened the household. Right away it was discovered that the jewelry was missing, and the ensuing din brought in the neighbors. A posse of men, equipped with lanterns and cudgels, took off after the thief.

I saw that the noble young altruist was quite shaken by what his guest had done, and so I took the opportunity to taunt him.

"You see what happens when you bring a guest home," I pointed out.

"So long as I live there'll be no more poor strangers in this house," he promised.

By this time the posse was busy searching the streets for the fugitive. They were joined by the night watch and the magistrate's constables. It wasn't very difficult to hunt down Reb Yomtov, lame and half-clothed as he was. They found him seated under a balcony, futilely attempting to set his dislocated ankle. Immediately they began to beat him with their clubs despite his protestations of innocence.

"Of course," they laughed, "innocent men always leave a house by the window in the middle of the night."

His hostess followed, screaming invectives at every step. "Thief! Murderer! Criminal! My jewels! My jewels!"

He kept repeating that he knew nothing about the robbery, but to no avail. The guards threw him into a cell and wrote down the names of the witnesses.

Glicka Genendel returned to bed. It was sweet to lie under the warm comforter while one's enemy rotted in jail. She thanked God for the favor he had bestowed upon her, and promised to donate eighteen groshen to charity. All the running about had exhausted her, and she longed for sleep, but I came to her and would not permit her to rest.

"Why such great elation?" I inquired. "Yes, he's in jail all right, but now you won't get a divorce from him. He'll tell everyone whose husband he is, and you and your whole family will be disgraced."

"What should I do?" she asked.

"He sent you a divorce by a messenger to Janov. Go to Janov and get the papers. First of all, you'll be rid of him. Secondly, if you're not here, you can't be called as a witness. And if you're not at the trial, who will believe his story? When the excitement is over, you can return."

My argument convinced her, and the very next morning she arose at sunrise, and explained to her daughter that she was off to Warsaw to meet her husband, Reb Yomtov. Her daughter was still in a state of shock and so did not put up much resistance. Actually Glicka Genendel wanted to put back the jewelry she had stolen from her daughter, but I talked her out of it.

"What's the rush?" I asked. "If the jewels are found, they'll let the liar out, and who's that going to harm, but you? Let him stay behind bars. He'll learn that one doesn't trifle with such a fine, upstanding woman as you."

So to make a long story short, Glicka Genendel set out for Janov, with the intention of either meeting the messenger there in person, or at least getting some clue as to his whereabouts. When she walked into the market place, everyone stared at her. They all knew about the messenger and the divorce papers. She sought out the rabbi and the rabbi's wife snubbed her; his daughter, who was the one who let her in, did not bid her welcome, nor ask her to sit down. But, at any rate, the rabbi gave her the facts: a messenger had come to Janov to present her with divorce papers, but not being able to locate her in town, had left. He remembered that the messenger was named Leib and that he came from Piask. Leib, he recalled, had yellow hair and a red beard. When Glicka Genendel heard this, she immediately engaged a carriage to take her to Piask. There was no point in staying in Janov any longer as the townspeople avoided her.

Reb Yomtov was still in jail. He sat surrounded by thieves and murderers. Vermin-infested rags were his only clothing. Twice daily he fed on bread and water.

And then, at length, the day of his trial rolled round, and he stood before the judge, who turned out to be an irascible man who was hard of hearing.

"Well, what about the jewels?" the judge growled. "Did you steal them?"

Reb Yomtov pleaded not guilty. He was no thief.

"All right, you're no thief. But why did you run out of the house in the middle of the night?"

"I was running away from my wife," Reb Yomtov explained.

"What wife?" the judge asked angrily.

Patiently Reb Yomtov began his elucidation: The mother-in-law of the man at whose house he had been staying was none other than his, Reb Yomtov's wife, but the judge did not allow him to proceed further.

"That's a fine story," he shouted. "You certainly are a brazen-faced liar."

Nevertheless, he did send for Glicka Genendel. Since she had already left town, her daughter came in her place, and testified that it was quite true that her mother was married, but that it was to a highly respectable man from Jerusalem, the famous scholar Reb Yomtov. As a matter of fact, she was even then on her way to meet him.

The prisoner lowered his eyes and cried out, "I am Reb Yomtov."

"You Reb Yomtov," the woman shouted. "Everyone knows you are Reb Solomon Simeon." And she began to curse him with the choicest oaths at her command.

"The farce is over," the judge said sternly. "We have enough scoundrels here already. We don't need any foreign importations." And he decreed that the prisoner be given twenty-five lashes, and then hanged.

It did not take long for the Jews of Lublin to hear of the decree; one of their own, and a scholar at that, was to be hanged, and immediately they sent a delegation to intercede with the governor in the prisoner's behalf. But this time they could accomplish nothing.

"Why are you Jews always so anxious to buy back your criminals?" the governor asked. "We know how to deal with ours, but you let yours off scot free. No wonder there are so many crooks among you." And he had the delegation chased off by dogs, and Reb Yomtov remained in jail.

He lay in his cell, chained hand and foot, awaiting execution. As he tossed about on his bundle of straw, mice darted out from chinks in the wall, and gnawed at his limbs. He cursed them and sent them scurrying back to cover. Outside the sun shone, but in his dungeon all was black as night. His situation, he saw, was comparable to that of the Prophet Jonah when he had been deep inside the stomach of the whale. He opened his lips to pray, but I, Satan the Destroyer, came to him and said, "Are you stupid enough to still believe in the power of prayer? Remember how the Jews prayed during the Black Plague, and, nevertheless, how they perished like flies? And what about the thousands the Cossacks butchered? There was enough prayer, wasn't there, when Chmielnicki came? How were those prayers answered? Children were buried alive, chaste wives raped—and later their bellies ripped open and cats sewed inside. Why should God bother with your prayers? He neither hears nor sees. There is no judge. There is no judgment."

This is the way I spoke to him, after the fashion of the philosophers, and shortly his lips had lost their inclination to pray.

"How can I save myself?" he asked. "What is your advice?"

"Become a convert," I told him. "Let the priests sprinkle a little holy water over you. That way you can stay alive and have revenge in the bargain. You do want to revenge yourself, don't you, on your enemies? And who are your enemies but the Jews, the Jews who are quite willing to see you hang because of the lies that a Jewess has invented to destroy you?"

He listened carefully to these words of wisdom and when the turnkey brought him his food, told him that he had a desire to be converted. This news was brought to the priests, and a monk was dispatched to interview the prisoner.

"What is your motive in wanting to become a Christian?" the monk inquired. "Is it merely to save your skin? Or has Jesus Christ entered your heart?"

It had happened while he was asleep, Reb Yomtov explained. His grandfather had come to him in a vision. Jesus, the saintly man had told him, was among the most exalted in Heaven, and sat with the Patriarchs in Paradise. No sooner did Reb Yomtov's words reach the bishop, than the prisoner was taken out of his cell, and washed and combed. Dressed in clean raiment, he was put in the company of a friar who instructed him in the catechism; and while he learned of the significance of the host and the cross, he dined on delicious food. What is more, the best families in the neighborhood came to visit him. Then, at last, he was led at the head of a procession to the monastery and converted to Christianity. Now he was certain that his troubles were over, and that he would shortly be a free man, but instead he was led back to his cell.

"When one is sentenced to death," the priest told him, "there's no way out. But don't be sorrowful; you will go with a clean soul into the next world."

Now Reb Yomtov realized that he had cut himself off from all of his worlds. His sorrow was so extreme that he lost his power of speech and spoke not one word as the hangman tightened the noose around his neck.

IV

On her way from Janov to Piask, Glicka Genendel stopped to visit a relative. She spent the Sabbath and Pentecost in the small village in which this relative lived. As she helped her hostess decorate the windows for the holiday, she munched on butter-cookies. And then the day after Pentecost she resumed her journey to Piask.

Of course, it never entered her mind that she was already a widow. Nor did it occur to her, you may be sure, that she was walking into a trap, a trap that I had baited. She traveled leisurely, stopping at all the inns on the way, stuffing herself with egg-cookies and brandy. She did not forget the coachman, but bought him egg-cookies and brandy as well, and to show his gratitude, he arranged a comfortable seat for her in the wagon, and helped her to mount and alight. He looked her over lecherously, but she couldn't bring herself to lie with so low a fellow.

The weather was mild. The fields were green with wheat. Storks circled overhead; frogs croaked, crickets chirped; butterflies were everywhere. At night as the wagon rolled through the deep forest, Glicka Genendel stretched herself out on the matting like a queen, and loosened her blouse, and permitted the soft breezes to cool her skin. She was well along in years, but her body had resisted old age, and passion still burnt in her as brightly as ever. Already she was making plans to get a new husband.

Then early one morning she arrived in Piask, just as the

merchants were opening their shops. The grass was still wet with dew. Troops of barefoot girls, carrying ropes and baskets, were on their way into the forest to gather firewood and mushrooms. Glicka Genendel sought out the assistant rabbi and asked him what he knew of her divorce. He received her cordially, explaining that the Bill of Divorcement had been drawn up by him personally and signed in his presence. The papers were now in the hands of Leib the Coachman. When Glicka Genendel suggested that the beadle be sent to fetch the man, the assistant rabbi made a counter proposal.

"Why don't you go to his house yourself?" he said. "Then you can settle the whole thing with him personally."

So Glicka Genendel went to Leib's house which was a hut that squatted on a hilltop behind the slaughterhouses. The roof of the building was made of rotting straw, and the windows were covered with cow-bladders instead of glass. Although it was summer, the earth around the house was wet and slimy, but this did not bother the ragged, half-naked children who were entertaining themselves there with worn-out brooms and poultry feathers. Scrawny goats, as grimy as pigs, scurried about this way and that.

Leib the Coachman had neither wife nor children. He was a short, broad-shouldered man, with large hands and feet; there was a growth on his forehead and his beard was a fiery red. He was dressed in a short jacket and straw shoes; on his head he wore the lining of a cap which could not quite conceal his bristling tufts of yellow hair.

The sight of him repelled Glicka Genendel, but, nevertheless, she said, "Are you Leib?"

"Well, we can be sure of one thing, you're not Leib," he answered insolently.

"Do you have the divorce papers?"

"What business is that of yours?" he wanted to know.

"I am Glicka Genendel. The divorce was drawn up for me."

"That's your story," he said. "How do I know you're telling me the truth? I don't see your name written on your forehead."

Glicka Genendel realized that this was going to be a difficult man to deal with, and she asked, "What's the matter? Are you after money?— Don't worry I'll give you a handsome tip."

"Come back tonight," he said.

And when she inquired why that was necessary, he told her that one of his horses was dying, and he couldn't bear any further conversation. He conducted her into an alleyway. There lay an emaciated nag with a mangy skin, foam frothing from its mouth, its stomach rising and falling like a bellows. Droves of flies buzzed around the dying creature, and overhead were circling crows, cawing as they waited.

"Very well, I'll come back this evening," Glicka Genendel said, now thoroughly disgusted. And her high buttoned shoes moved as fast as she could make them go, taking her away from the ruin and poverty.

It just happened that the night before the Piask thieves had been out on business; they had invaded Lenchic with carts and covered wagons, and had emptied the stores. It had been the evening before market day and so there had been more than enough goods to take. But this rich haul had not been sufficient to satisfy the raiders; they had also broken into the church and had divested it of its gold chains, crowns, plates, and jewels. The holy statues had been left naked. Then they had beaten a hasty retreat homewards, and, as a matter of fact, the horse that Glicka Genendel had seen expiring had been a casualty of the expedition; it had been whipped so mercilessly during the withdrawal that it had collapsed as soon as the robbers had reached home.

Of course, Glicka Genendel knew nothing of this. She went to an inn and ordered a roast chicken. To get the sight of the dying horse out of her mind, she drank a pint of mead. Inevitably, she made friends with all the male guests, inquiring of each his name, home town, and business in this vicinity. Inevitably also, she spoke of her background: her noble descent, her knowledge of Hebrew, her wealth, her jewels, her skill at cooking, sewing, and crocheting. Then when dinner was finished she went to her room and took a nap.

She awoke to find that the sun was setting and that the cows were being driven home from pasture. From the chimneys of the village smoke was issuing as the housewives prepared the evening meal.

Once more Glicka Genendel took the path that led to Leib's. When she entered the house she left behind the purple dusk, and found herself in a night that was almost as black as the inside of a chimney. There was only one small candle burning—inside of a shard. She could just make out Leib who sat astride an inverted bucket. He was mending a saddle. Leib was not a thief himself; he just drove for the thieves.

Glicka Genendel began to talk business immediately, and he took up his old complaint. "How do I know that it's your divorce?"

"Here take these two gulden and stop this nonsense," she said.

"It's not a question of money," he grumbled.

"What's eating you, anyway?" she wanted to know.

He hesitated for a moment.

"I am a man too," he said, "not a dog. I like the same things everyone else does." And he winked lecherously and pointed toward a bench-bed heaped with straw. Glicka Genendel was almost overcome with disgust, but I, the Prince of Darkness, hastened to whisper in her ear, "It doesn't pay to haggle with such an ignoramus."

She begged him to give her the divorce papers first. It was merely a question of lessening the sin. Didn't he see that it would be better for all concerned if he went to bed with a divorcee rather than a married woman? But he was too shrewd for that.

"Oh, no," he said, "as soon as I serve you with the papers, you'll change your mind."

He bolted the door and put out the candle. She wanted to scream but I muffled her voice. Oddly enough she was only half afraid; the other half of her was alive with lust. Leib pulled her down onto the straw; he stank of leather and horses. She lay there in silence and astonishment.

That such a thing should happen to me! she marveled to herself.

She did not know that it was I, the Arch-Fiend, who stoked her blood and muddled her reason. Outside destruction already lay in wait for her.

Suddenly there was the sound of horsemen. The door was splintered open as if by a hurricane, and dragoons and guardsmen, carrying torches, burst into the room. All this happened so quickly that the adulterers did not even get a chance to stop what they were doing. Glicka Genendel screamed and fainted.

This foray had been led by the Lenchic squire himself who came with his troops to punish the thieves. His men broke into the homes of all known criminals. An informer accompanied the platoon. Leib wilted at the first blow and confessed that he was a driver for the gang. Two soldiers hustled him out, but before they left one of them asked Glicka Genendel, "Well, whore, who are you?"

And he ordered that she be searched.

Of course, she protested that she knew nothing of the sacking of Lenchic, but the informer said, "Don't listen to that tart!" He thrust his hand inside her bosom and drew out a treasure trove: her daughter's jewelry and Reb Yomtov's pouch of gold. Under the glow of the torches, the ducats, diamonds, sapphires, and rubies gleamed wickedly. Now Glicka Genendel could not doubt that misfortune had overtaken her, and she threw herself at the squire's feet, begging for mercy. But despite her entreaties she was clapped into irons and taken along with the other thieves to Lenchic.

At her trial, she swore that the jewels were her own. But the rings did not fit her fingers, nor the bracelets her wrists. She was asked how much money was in the pouch, but she did not know because Reb Yomtov had coins from Turkey in his hoard. When the prosecutor wanted to know where she had obtained the ducats, she replied, "From my husband."

"And where is your husband?"

"In Lublin," she blurted out in her confusion, "in prison."

"The husband is a jailbird," the prosecutor said. "And she is a whore. The jewelry is obviously not hers, and she doesn't even know how much money is in her possession. Is there any doubt about the conclusion?"

Everyone agreed that there was not.

Now Glicka Genendel saw that her chances were indeed slim, and it occurred to her that her only hope was to announce that she had a daughter and son-in-law in Lublin, and that the jewelry belonged to her daughter. But I said to her, "First of all, no one's going to believe you. And suppose they do, look what happens. They fetch your daughter here and she finds out that not only have you stolen her jewelry, but also that you've fornicated with that scab-head like a common harlot. The disgrace will kill her, and so you'll have your punishment anyway. Incidentally, Reb Yomtov will be released, and believe me, he'll find your situation amusing. No, better keep quiet. Rather perish than yield to your enemies."

And although my advice led to the abyss, she did not object, for it is well known that my people are vain and will lay down their lives for their vanity. For what is the pursuit of pleasure but pride and delusion?

So Glicka Genendel was sentenced to the gallows.

The night before the execution I came to her and urged her to become a convert, just as I had in the case of the late, unlamented Reb Yomtov, but she said, "Is it any greater honor to have a convert for a mother than a prostitute? No, I'll go to my death a good Jewess."

Don't think I didn't do my best! I pleaded with her over and over again, but, as it is written: A female has nine measures of stubbornness.

The following day, a gallows was erected in Lenchic. When the town's Jews learned that a daughter of Israel was to be hanged, they became frantic and petitioned the Squire. But a church had been pillaged, and he would not grant mercy. And so from the surrounding areas the peasants and gentry drove in, converging on the place of execution in coaches and wagons. Hog-butchers hawked salamis. Beer and whiskey were guzzled.

A darkness fell upon the Jews, and they closed their shutters at mid-day. Just before the execution, there was a near-riot among the peasants as to who would stand closest to the gallows in order to get a piece of the rope for a good luck charm.

First they hanged the thieves, Leib the Coachman among

them. Then Glicka Genendel was led up the steps. Before the hood was placed over her head, they asked her if she had a final request, and she begged that the rabbi be summoned to hear her confession. He came, and she told him the true story. It was probably the first time in her life she had ever told the truth. The rabbi recited the Confession for her and promised her Paradise.

It seems, however, that the Lenchic rabbi had little influence in Heaven because before Glicka Genendel and Reb Yomtov were admitted to Paradise, they had to atone for every last sin. No allowances are made up there for anything.

When I told this story to Lilith, she found it very amusing and decided to see these two sinners in Gehenna. I flew with her to purgatory and showed her how they hung suspended by their tongues, which is the prescribed punishment for liars. Under their feet were braziers of burning hot coals. Devils flogged their bodies with fiery rods. I called out to the sinners, "Now, tell me whom did you fool with those lies? Well, you have only yourselves to thank. Your lips spun the thread, and your mouths wove the net. But be of good cheer. Your stay in Gehenna lasts only for twelve months, including Sabbaths and holidays."

Translated from the Yiddish
by Cecil Hemley and
June Ruth Flaum

The Shadow of a Crib

I

DR. YARETZKY'S ARRIVAL

All of a sudden, one day, a new doctor came to town. He arrived in a hired wagon, with a basket of possessions, a stack of books bound with a thong, a parrot in a cage and a poodle. In his thirties, short, swarthy, with black eyes and mustache, he might have looked Jewish, if his nose had not had its Polish tilt. He wore an elegant, old-fashioned fur-lined overcoat, gaiters, and a broad-brimmed hat like those of gypsies, magicians and tinkers. Standing amid his things in the center of the market place, he addressed the Jews in the halting Yiddish a gentile occasionally acquires: "Hey there,

Jews, I want to live here. Me, Doctor. Doctor Yaretzky. . . .
Head hurt, eh? See tongue!"

"Where are you from?" the Jews asked.

"Far, far away! . . ."

"A madman!" the Jews decided, "A mad doctor!"

He settled in a house on a side street, near the fields. He had neither wife, nor furniture. He bought an iron bed and a rickety table. The old doctor, Chwaschinski, charged fifty groszy per visit and a half-ruble for outside calls, but Dr. Yaretzky took what was offered, jamming it uncounted into his pocket. He liked to joke with his patients. Soon two factions formed in town—those who insisted he was a quack who did not know his foot from his elbow, and others who swore he was a master physician. One glance at a patient, his admirers claimed, and diagnosis was complete. He restored the dying to life.

The apothecary, the mayor appointed by the Russians, the notary public and the Russian authorities were all partisan to Dr. Chwaschinski. Since Yaretzky did not attend church, the priest maintained that the doctor was no Christian but an infidel, perhaps a Tartar—and a heathen. Some suggested that he might even poison people. He could be a sorcerer. But the destitute Jews of Bridge Street and the sand flats patronized Dr. Yaretzky. And the peasants too began to consult him, and Dr. Yaretzky furnished an office and hired a maid. But he still wore disheveled clothes and remained friendless. Alone, he strolled down oak-lined Zamosc Avenue. Alone he shopped for groceries, since his maid was a deaf-mute who could neither write nor haggle. In fact, she rarely left the house at all.

The maid was rumored pregnant. Her belly began to expand—but eventually flattened again. Yaretzky was blamed for both the pregnancy and the miscarriage. The authorities at their club spoke of putting the doctor on trial, but the prosecutor was a timid man, afraid of the piercing black eyes and satanic smile beneath Yaretzky's bristling mustache. Yaretzky had, moreover, a medical diploma from Petersburg, and, since he feared no one, possibly had influence with the aristocracy. When visiting Jewish homes, he derided Dr. Chwaschinski, called the apothecary a sucking leech, maligned the County Natchalnik, the Town Natchalnik, the Post Natchalnik, branded them thieves, boot-lickers, lackeys. He even taught obscenities to the parrot. How could anyone start a feud with him? Toward what end? Difficult childbirths were his stock in trade. If necessary, he operated. He lanced abscesses and malignancies unceremoniously, with a knife. They called him a butcher; nevertheless, they recovered. Dr. Chwaschinski was old—his hands trembled, his head shook from side to side, and he had grown deaf. His frequent illnesses forced people to go to Yaretzky. When the mayor was his patient, Dr. Yaretzky addressed him in Yiddish as if that dignitary were a Jew.

"Head hurt? Aah—tongue!" and he tickled the mayor under the arm.

The Doctor conducted himself even more outrageously with the women. Before they could say what was wrong, he made them disrobe. Pipe in mouth, he blew smoke into their faces. Once during conscription time, when Dr. Chwaschinski was sick, Dr. Yaretzky became the assistant to the military doctor, an elderly colonel from Lublin, who was forever drunk. Dr. Yaretzky let the Jewish population know that for one hundred rubles he would issue a blue certificate, signifying rejection during peacetime, for two hundred—a white, meaning absolute rejection, and for a five-and-twenty note, a green—a postponement for at least a year's duration. Mothers of indigent recruits came weeping to Yaretzky and he'd lower the price for them. That year, scarcely a Jew was drafted into the service. An informer was sent to Lublin and a military commission arrived to investigate, but Dr. Yaretzky was exonerated. No doubt he bribed the commission or fooled them completely. In Jewish homes he would say: "Mother Russia is a pig, no? She stinks!"

After Dr. Chwaschinski's death the gentry began to try to please Dr. Yaretzky. The mayor pledged a truce with him, the apothecary invited him to a party. The ladies praised his gifts as an *accoucheur*.

Mrs. Woychehovska, a stout person who, morning and evening walked to church wearing a black shawl over her head and carrying a gold-embossed prayer book, was a gentile marriage broker in the town. Mrs. Woychehovska kept a roster of eligible bachelors and maidens. She frequented the better homes. She boasted that her matches were arranged in dreams by an angel who appeared revealing who was destined for whom. To date, not one of her couples had ever quarreled, separated or proved childless.

Mrs. Woychehovska came to Dr. Yaretzky proposing a highly advantageous match. The young lady came from one of the noblest families in Poland. Her widowed mother owned an estate just outside town. Although Helena was no longer in the first flush of youth, she was single; not from lack of suitors, but from overdiscrimination, Mrs. Woychehovska assured Dr. Yaretzky. She had picked and chosen for so long, that she had been left a maiden. Helena was an accomplished pianist, could converse in French and read poetry. She was known for her love of animals, she kept an aquarium of goldfish in her blue room, and had raised a pair of parrots on the farm. A donkey purchased from a licorice-selling Turk was in her stable. Mrs. Woychehovska swore to Dr. Yaretzky that in her dream she had seen him kneeling alongside Helena before the altar in church. Over their heads hung a halo emanating rays of light—a sure omen that they'd been destined for each other. Dr. Yaretzky heard her out, patiently.

"Who sent you?" he asked her after she'd finished, "the mother or the daughter?"

"For the love of Jesus, neither of them even suspects."

"Why bring Jesus into this?" Dr. Yaretzky said. "Jesus was nothing but a lousy Jew . . ."

Mrs. Woychehovska's face immediately flooded with tears. "Kind sir, what are you saying? May God forgive you! . . ."

"There is no God!"

"Then what is there?"

"Worms. . . ."

"Poor soul, I pity you! And may God pity you! He is merciful. He has compassion even for those who profane Him. . . ."

Mrs. Woychehovska left and crossed Dr. Yaretzky's name off her list. Soon afterwards she suffered an attack of hiccups and it was some time before the spasms subsided.

II

HELENA SEEKS REVENGE

Mrs. Woychehovska repeated the incident to her crony, a Mrs. Markewich who told it secretly to her in-law, a Mrs. Krul. Mrs. Krul's servant girl repeated it to a milkmaid who worked at the estate, and she in turn told it to Helena as her mistress was feeding bread and sugar to her pet donkey. Helena, normally pale, turned white as the lumps of sugar when she learned of the incident. She ran to her mother screaming: "Mama, I'll never forgive you for this, not even on my deathbed!"

The widow denied any knowledge of the affair, but Helena

was unconvinced. She flew to her blue room and ordered the chamber maid to remove the aquarium. She wanted to be alone, without the presence of even the goldfish. Bolting the door, closing the shutters, she began to pace up and down. Helena had suffered much. The day her father hanged himself from an apple tree in the orchard was the most terrible day of her life, but even that had been easier to bear than this. Dr. Yaretzky, that barbarian, that anti-Christ, that worm, had slapped her face, sullied her soul. If her servant knew, it must be common gossip by now. True, her mother swore she had not sent the matchmaker, but who would believe it? She, Helena, had been disgraced. The entire neighborhood was probably laughing at her.

But what could she do about it? Should she vanish so completely no one would ever hear of her again? Should she drown herself in the pond? Should she revenge herself upon that charlatan, Yaretzky?— But how? Were she a man, she would challenge him to a duel, but what could a mere female do? Fury raged in Helena's heart. Her honor had been the only thing left of her pride. Now, that too had been taken away. She'd been debased. There was nothing to do but die.

She stopped eating. She no longer fed the parrots and the donkey. She neglected to change the water in the fish tank. Naturally slim, she grew emaciated: a tall pale girl with a white face, a high forehead, and faded hair, once the color of gold, now like straw. White hairs became evident. Her skin grew transparent, networks of bluish veins covered her temples. Malnutrition and vexation sapped her strength, and she spent her days on the divan. Even Slowacki's divine poetry ceased to interest her.

When her mother realized that her only daughter was declining, she decided to act. But Helena refused to visit an aunt in Pietrkow Province. Nor would she consult doctors in

Lublin or vacation at the Nalenchow spa. Every night she tossed sleepless in bed, seeking ways to revenge herself on Yaretzky. The hot blood of her father, the squire, and other noble ancestors tormented her. She fancied herself an avenging knight, stripping Yaretzky and lashing him in the market-square. After the scourging, she bound him to the tail of a pack horse and had him dragged off to the turnpike. And then, after all this torture, she gouged bits of flesh from his body and poured acid into the wounds. And while she was at it, she had that accursed matchmaker, that Woychehovska slut hanged.

But what good were fantasies? They merely fatigued the mind and intensified one's helplessness.

III
HELENA ATTENDS A BALL

Who can understand the feminine soul? Even an angelic woman shelters within herself devils, imps, and goblins. The evil ones act perversely, mock human feelings, profane holiness. For example, in Shebreshin during a funeral oration over a deceased landlord, a Squire Woyski, his widow suddenly burst out laughing. She stood over the coffin and laughed so intemperately that all the mourners and even the deceased's relatives began to laugh with her. Another time in Zamosc the wife of a brewer went to a barber-surgeon to have a tooth pulled, and when the man put his finger in her mouth to test the tooth, the woman bit it. Afterwards she began to wail and suffered an epileptic fit. Such things happen frequently. It is all part of the perversity so characteristic of the female's nature.

It happened this way. The Post Natchalnik, a Russian married to a Pole, the daughter of a squire near Hrubyeshov, gave a ball to celebrate his wife's birthday. He invited the entire officialdom, as well as the better Polish townspeople and the neighboring gentry, Helena and her mother included. In the past, Helena had always found some excuse to avoid these social functions. Years passed without a single formal appearance on her part. But this time she decided to go. Her mother was overjoyed. She summoned Aaron-Leib, the most successful ladies' tailor in town, and gave him a bolt of silk from which to fashion a ball gown for her daughter. The material had been lying around for years. Aaron-Leib took Helena's measurements and complimented her on her slenderness. Most of the ladies were squat and chunky and the clothes looked baggy on them. This was the first time Helena had permitted a man to touch her. In the past, it had been almost impossible to take her measurements, but this time she cooperated. She was even amiable to this Jew, Aaron-Leib, and asked about his family. Before he left, she gave him a coin for his youngest daughter. Aaron-Leib thanked God for having left him off so easily. Helena's reputation was that of an eccentric.

Customarily Helena accepted an invitation only after having made a full inquiry into the lists of guests. She kept a mental dossier on everybody. This one didn't please her, the other was beneath her station, a third had done a disservice to her father, or grandfather—she found fault with everyone. Quite often, if the hostess wanted Helena to attend, she was forced to scratch some prospective guests off her list, but, if on the other hand, she refused to give in, Helena grew enraged and severed all relations with the person. This time, however, Helena made no stipulations. She seemed to have forgotten her previous misanthropy; her feminine vanity had awakened. She insisted on several fittings of her gown, she ordered dancing slippers from Lublin, and each day she tried on a new item of jewelry to see what would be most appropriate. She grew sprightlier, more talkative, her appetite sharpened, she slept more easily. Her mother was delighted. How long, after all, should a girl sulk and isolate herself? Perhaps God had heeded the widow's supplications and turned her daughter's heart towards conventional behavior. The widow's hopes for the ball were high. Besides the married men, several eligible bachelors were to attend. Two orchestras had been engaged, one military, the other civilian.

Helena, when younger, had been considered an excellent dancer, but she hadn't danced in years, and new dances were in vogue. She asked her mother to hire the town dancemaster, Professor Rayanc. He came and gave Helena lessons. The servants stared as Mistress Helena whirled around the salon with the lanky Professor, who it was said, was ill with consumption and wore a wig to cover his bald head. He was astonished at how quickly Helena learned the new steps. His black eyes filled with tears of admiration, and he suffered a coughing spell, spitting blood into a silken handkerchief. The widow offered him a glass of cherry brandy and a bit of pastry. He licked his fingers and raised the glass: "To your health, esteemed Ladies! May you soon dance at Lady Helena's wedding!"

And he artfully twirled the button on his highly lacquered shoe to make sure the toast would become a reality.

The gown turned out more beautiful than expected. It fit Helena as if she'd been made for it. The flower on the shoulder strap and the gold tasseled bow about the waist lent the gown a chic and elegance rare even in the large cities.

The day of the ball was sunny and the evening mild. Britzskas, carriages and phaetons pulled up before the officer's club where the balls were held. Horses and vehicles filled the parade ground where the soldiers drilled. Liveried footmen mingled with common coachmen. Ladies in sweeping gowns splendid with tucks and ribbons, escorted by gentlemen in dress-uniforms and civilian evening attire with rows of medals on their chests, tried to outshine each other. An old Polish nobleman with mustachios extending to his shoulders accompanied his small round wife, who carried a fringed umbrella even though the sky was clear. Regimental caps and swords hung in the hall. Many young people of the town had assembled around the club to watch the guests and listen to the dance music. The horses behaved as always—chewing their oats and swishing their tails. Occasionally one would whinny but the others disregarded him. What did a horse's whinny mean? Nothing—even to horses.

Helena and her mother arrived late, after the music had started. When the coachman opened the carriage door and Helena stepped down she was greeted by the admiring shrieks of the girls and whistles of the young hoodlums. She was like a portrait come alive.

IV
A KISS ON THE HAND

Helena and her mother were welcomed by the Post Natchalnik and his wife. Other guests came to greet them. The men kissed their hands, the ladies paid them compliments. Helena felt as if she were floating. She spoke, not knowing what she said, or why. Her eyes searched, not knowing for whom. Suddenly she spied Dr. Yaretzky. He was surrounded by young, attractive ladies—the wives and daughters of the gentry and the authorities. He might have been the only man in the ballroom who wore no medals. The days when Yaretzky had been branded gypsy, Jew-barber and Devil were long past. The town's ladies, particularly the young and prominent ones, adored him. They repeated his piquant witticisms, they lauded his medical ability. They even forgave him his bachelorhood and his living with the deaf-mute servant girl. He was bold with the ladies, having delivered the children of some and seen others undressed in his office.

When Helena saw him, she was stunned momentarily. She had almost forgotten about him—or had she made herself forget? He seemed so dashing now in his dress coat and highly polished shoes. The black eyes seemed wise and humorous. A young woman tried coquettishly to place a flower in his lapel where apparently there was no buttonhole. The women laughed and clapped their hands, as Dr. Yaretzky undoubtedly offered a riposte, one of his impertinent sallies, which no other man present would have dared utter in mixed company. "Do I still hate him?" Helena asked herself, and even as she asked it, she knew the answer. Her antagonism had mysteriously dissolved—and been replaced by a curiosity as strong as her enmity—perhaps even stronger. She realized something else: she had not forgotten about Dr. Yaretzky at all but had thought of him constantly, possessed as if in a dream, when one thinks with every tissue of the brain without being aware of it. "Will someone introduce us?" she wondered. "I must speak with him, dance with him."

She was jealous of the fawning women who flirted with him so casually. As if he'd been reading her mind, the Natchalnik said: "Is the esteemed Lady Helena acquainted with our Doctor Yaretzky? One moment, if you please. . . ."

He trotted over to Yaretzky, whispered something in his ear, took him by the arm and good-naturedly led him over to Helena.

The other ladies protested, half jestingly, that he was appropriating their cavalier. A few of them even trailed along, not sure of how to react. The balmy evening, the scintillating music, the fragrance of the flowers and perfumes and the drinks the ladies had had, all contributed to an atmosphere of frivolity; Yaretzky bowed to Helena, his smoldering eyes seemed to imply: "Yes, it's about time we two got together. I've anticipated this meeting!" and he offered his hand.

And then there occurred one of those mysteries, one of those imponderables, which confound human reason. Helena lifted Dr. Yaretzky's hand to her mouth—and kissed it. It happened so quickly, that she did not realize what she had done until afterwards. She laughed strangely. Her mother choked off a scream. The ladies were struck dumb. The Natchalnik looked paralyzed—his mouth remained open. Only two young officers began to hoot and clap their palms along their striped trousers. Dr. Yaretzky himself turned pale, but quickly recovered and said: "If Mohammed does not come to the mountain, the mountain comes to Mohammed. . . . Since I neglected to kiss Lady Helena's hand, the Lady kissed mine," and he took Helena's hand and kissed it three times, twice on the glove and once on the exposed wrist. Only now did the ladies begin to titter, prattle. In a second, the story had spread through the ballroom. The guests found it incredible. Everyone was overcome with curiosity and a sense of scandal. The town would have something to gossip about for months to come. Even the lackeys, coachmen and servant girls outside quickly learned of the incident. Their eyes widened. Was she insane? Was she madly infatuated with him? Had someone bewitched her? The musicians came to life, as if revived by the indiscretion and both orchestras began to play with renewed vigor. The violins sang, the bass fiddles buzzed, the cellos shrieked, the trumpets wailed, the drums throbbed. The dancers' feet grew light, reacting with satisfaction to the spectacle of another's downfall. A debauched mood infected everyone. Couples previously inhibited now danced into the corridors or the courtyard and openly embraced. If Helena could kiss Dr. Yaretzky's hand before everyone, what need was there for decorum?

In ten minutes the widow and Helena had left the ball. Her mother held her train in one hand and pulled Helena along with the other. Helena did not walk but shuffled slightly. The coachmen snickered, pointed, whispered a muffled innuendo. The widow's coachman quickly came up to help the ladies into their carriage. The widow could not raise her feet and the coachman had to lift her up by her hips. Helena collapsed into the carriage. The driver mounted, cracked his whip and a great cry came up from everyone—catcalls, hooting. Children who should have been asleep mingled with the adults, running behind the carriage, screaming frenziedly, flinging stones and horse dung. Someone at the ball had overheard the widow admonish Helena: "Wretched girl, what can you do now but dig a grave and lie down in it?"

After the widow and Helena had left, the ladies flocked around Dr. Yaretzky with increased enthusiasm. They chattered, smiled, lured him with their eyes, as if each were Helena's mortal enemy, and savored her disgrace. They tried to extract from Dr. Yaretzky a word, an explanation, a passing remark, even a jest—anything that could be repeated later. Dr. Yaretzky seemed perturbed, his face pallid. Without either answering or apologizing, he forced his way past those who surrounded him. He left the ballroom, not through the main entrance, but through a side door. Since he lived near the club, he'd come on foot, and now he headed home. Someone against whom he happened to stumble maintained that the Doctor had not been walking, but running.

Alone at last in his office, Dr. Yaretzky asked aloud: "Now, what sort of nonsense was that?"

He did not light his kerosene lamp, but sat on the couch in

the dark. Since his arrival in town he'd enjoyed many triumphs, but today's conquest was not to his taste. Obviously, Helena was madly in love with him, but to what end? She was no eager matron, simply an old maid. He had no desire to saddle himself with a wife, to become a father and to raise sons and daughters—to perpetrate all that absurdity. He had his share of money and affairs. On this same couch he'd experienced adventures which would have been branded pathological lies by him, had they been claimed by someone else. Long ago he had concluded that family life was a fraud, a swamp to mire fools—since deceit is as essential to women as violence to men. It was not too likely that Helena would deceive him, but what use was she to him? He appealed to women because he was single. As soon as a man marries, other women treat him like a leper. "I'll ignore the incident," Dr. Yaretzky decided. "They'll gossip about it until they forget it. Every scandal grows stale eventually."

He went into the bedroom and lay down—but sleep would not come. He could still hear the music from the ball—polkas, mazurkas, military marches. Distant laughter and sounds of violence drifted towards him. A warm breeze bore the scents of grass, leaves, flowers from beneath his window. Crickets chirped, frogs croaked. The night swarmed with myriads of creatures, each of them calling. Dogs bayed, cats caterwauled. A neighbor's child awoke in its crib. The moon, obscured earlier, now appeared, suspended miraculously in the sky. Stars of many colors sparkled around it. "What is it she sees in me? Why is her love so strong?" mused Dr. Yaretzky. "It's only that old urge to reproduce." The Doctor considered himself a follower of Schopenhauer. No one understood the truth as well as that pessimistic philosopher. His collected works, bound in leather, tooled in gold, stood in Dr. Yaretzky's bookcase. Yes, it was only the blind will to propagate, to perpetuate suffering, the eternal human tragedy. But for what purpose? Why give in to the will if one were aware of its blindness? Man was given his drop of intellect so that he might expose the instincts and their devices.

The Doctor realized that it was useless to try to sleep. He was even out of the sleeping pills he had taken on similar nights. He put on his clothes. He suddenly felt like walking. It might help him sleep later.

V

A WINDOW IN THE RABBI'S STUDY

Dr. Yaretzky walked without knowing where. Did it matter? He felt unusually alert and agile. His feet hadn't seemed this light in years. He observed that although this day's triumph had only embarrassed him, his nervous system reacted as it had to previous triumphs. His body felt buoyant as if Helena's kiss on his hand had diminished the effect of gravity. He breathed more deeply. His senses grew keener. "If I were to go hunting right now," he thought, "I could trap a stag with my bare hands. I'd grab him by his antlers and snap his spine." He felt an urge to fire a gun but had left his revolver at home. He wanted to rap on a shutter and frighten a Jew—but controlled himself. After all, a doctor couldn't behave like a wanton boy.

Yaretzky grew more serious. He recalled that afternoon, years ago, when, having divided a sheet of paper into many slips, each bearing the name of a county seat, he had picked from a hat the name of this town. What if he had picked another town? Would his life have been different? Consequently, everything that had happened to him had been pure chance. But what, actually, was chance? If everything was predetermined, no such thing as chance existed. And then again, if causality was nothing but a category of reason, then there certainly was no such thing as chance. The thought swiftly went further. Conceding that Schopenhauer was right, then that which Kant called "The thing in itself" was will. But how did it follow that the will was blind? If the world-will could bring out Schopenhauer's intellect, why couldn't the world-will itself be endowed with intelligence? "I'll have to consult 'The World as Will and Idea'," Dr. Yaretzky decided. "There's bound to be some sort of an answer in there. I've neglected my reading shamelessly."

He realized that he was in the street, near the rabbi's house. A shutter in the rabbi's study was open. On a table near the stove, a candle flickered in a brass candleholder. Books and manuscripts were heaped on the table. The venerable rabbi, his white beard distended, a skull cap above his high forehead, an unbuttoned gabardine over a yellow-gray fringed garment, sat engrossed in a book, glass of tea in hand. On one side of him was a samovar, on the other, a fan of chicken feathers, used no doubt to fan the coals. Everything, it seemed, was precisely where it should be. The old rabbi was pouring over one of his theological volumes, but Dr. Yaretzky watched, amazed. Did the rabbi keep such late hours, or had he already risen for the day? And what in that book engrossed him so much? The rabbi seemed withdrawn from the world. The Doctor knew the old man. He had treated him for catarrh and hemorrhoids. He, Yaretzky, had handled the rabbi with more respect than the other patients, had not said: "Say aah—," had not asked: "Head hurt, eh? . . ." The Jews of the town deified their rabbi, spoke of his erudition. His large gray eyes, his high forehead, his entire appearance suggested knowledge, understanding, character—and yet something else, reminiscent of an alien, impenetrable culture. It was too bad that the rabbi knew neither Polish nor Russian, for Yaretzky, while he had learned a little Yiddish in his youth, did not understand it sufficiently to converse with the rabbi. The old man seemed more spiritual than ever now. Blending with the night, he resembled an ancient sage, both saint and philosopher—a Hebrew Socrates or Diogenes. His shadow extended to the ceiling. "Where do they get such huge foreheads?" Yaretzky wondered. He remembered what the other Jews had told him—that the rabbi was a *gaon*, a genius. But what kind of a genius? Only in line with prescribed dogma? And how could he have made peace with a world full of sorrow? "I'd give one hundred rubles to know what the old man is reading!" Yaretzky said to himself. "One thing is certain—he doesn't even know there's a ball tonight. Physically they dwell side by side with us, but spiritually they are somewhere in Palestine, on Mount Sinai or God knows where. He may not even be aware that this is the Nineteenth Century. Surely he doesn't know that he is in Europe. He exists beyond time and space. . . ."

Yaretzky recalled something he'd read in a periodical: The Jews do not record their history, they have no sense of chronology. It would seem that instinctively they know that time and space are mere illusion. If that were so, perhaps they could break through the categories of pure reason and conceive the thing-in-itself, that which is behind phenomena?

Yaretzky's urge to communicate with the rabbi increased. He stopped himself just as he was about to tap on the window. He knew beforehand that he would be unable to speak with the old man.— Who knows? Perhaps it was their desire to remain apart that kept them from learning other languages. Judaism could be summed up in one word:—isolation. If not driven into a ghetto, Jews formed a ghetto voluntarily; if not compelled to display a yellow patch, they wore the kind of clothes that their neighbors found odd.

On the other hand, the Jews who did learn other languages and mingled with the Christians were bores.

VI
A SCENE OF LOVE

Just as he was about to walk on, something else caught his eye. The door opened from a back room and an old woman, entered, tiny, with bent shoulders, dressed in a wide housecoat and battered slippers. Rather than walk, she scraped along—the bent head bound in a kerchief, the face puckered as a cabbage leaf, the ancient eyes hung with pouches. She crept towards the table, silently picked up the chicken feather fan and fanned the coals under the samovar. Dr. Yaretzky knew her well. It was the rabbi's wife. Strange, that the rabbi did not address her and kept his eyes on the book. But his face grew gentler as he half-concentrated on his reading, half-listened to his wife's movements. He raised his eyebrows and on the ceiling the shadow trembled. Dr. Yaretzky stood there, unable to move. He was convinced that he witnessed a love-scene, an old, pious, love ritual between husband and wife. She'd roused herself in the middle of the night to tend the coals of the rabbi's samovar. He, the rabbi, did not dare interrupt his holy studies but, aware of her nearness, he offered silent gratitude. How different all this was! How oriental!—"They've lived for no one knows how many years in Europe. Their great-great-great-grandfathers were born here, but they conduct themselves as if only yesterday they'd been exiled from Jerusalem. How is this possible? Is such behavior hereditary? Or is this an expression of deep faith? How can they be so certain that everything inscribed in several ancient volumes is absolutely true?

"Well, and what of me? How can I guarantee that the world

is blind will? Let us say, for the sake of argument that 'The thing in itself' is not blind will, but a seeing will. Then the whole concept of the cosmos changes. Because, if the universal powers are capable of seeing, then they see all—every person, every worm, every atom, every thought. Then the slip of paper that I ostensibly chose by pure chance was not chosen by chance at all but was simply part of a plan, a decree that I experience everything that I've experienced here. If this is so, everything has a purpose: every insect, every blade of grass, every embryo in every mother's womb. It would then follow that that which Helena did tonight was no idle caprice, but part of a scheme of the all-seeing will. But just what is this scheme? Was I destined to become a father?"

It suddenly struck Dr. Yaretzky that while he'd been philosophizing, someone had lowered the curtain—he'd undoubtedly been observed. He felt ashamed. It would be gossiped about among the Jews that he loitered at windows.

He began to stride away hastily, almost running. His thoughts ran with him. He remembered that when he'd first come to town, the rabbi's beard had been blond, not white, and the rabbi's wife?—she'd still had a houseful of youngsters to raise. Had so many years passed? Does one change this quickly from youth to old age? And how old was he, Yaretzky? Would he too soon grow gray? And how long does life last? If it were true what he'd recently read in a medical magazine, he had fourteen years of life left. But how long is fourteen years? The past fourteen years had flown by like a dream. He couldn't exactly say where.

Something within Dr. Yaretzky began to rebel. "Is this my fate? Is this my purpose? Fourteen more years to creep to patients, then fall dead like a dray horse? How can I resign myself to this? No, better a bullet in the temple! But, conceding that the world-will is not blind—this opens innumerable possibilities. An all-seeing Will—is God. The rabbi, this would mean, is no fanatic at all. He has his philosophy. He believes in a seeing universe, rather than a blind one. All the rest is tradition, folklore. Apparently the powers of creation try to achieve variety in the shapes of their creatures, as well as in their behavior.

"Assuming this to be true, what must I do? Return to the church? Become a Jew? Stop seducing my patients? Because if the cosmos sees all, it can also punish. . . . No, I must put all this nonsense out of my head. From here on, it's but one more step to religious positivism. —But why am I running like this? And where?" All at once Dr. Yaretzky saw that he was at the widow's estate. His feet seemed to have brought him here of their own volition. "What am I doing? What am I looking for? Someone will surely see me! Am I going out of my mind?" But even while cautioning himself, he walked up to the gate leading into the courtyard. There was no watchman about, and the gate was unlocked. Unhesitatingly, he pushed it open and walked inside. "Suppose the dogs attack me? They'll mistake me for a prowler." Incautious, abandoned, he was like a drunk to whom awareness of his condition does not bring sobriety. He walked stealthily, like a boy raiding an orchard. He was searching for something, he did not know what.

Why were the dogs so still? Were they sleeping? Everything had been left unattended . . . The house emerged, its windows black. "She isn't here!" something within him said. He followed the path which led to the back of the house, the garden and the fields. Dr. Yaretzky had once visited the estate to treat an ailing farm hand, a long time ago. Although the moon was still shining, there was a pre-dawn silence in the air. The frogs and crickets grew still. The trees seemed petrified. The world held its breath, awaiting daybreak. Dr. Yaretzky felt as if everything within him had also ceased to function. He moved like a phantom. He was awake, but dreaming. He walked past a barn, sheds, a stack of hay. Suddenly he heard a moan and at that instant a shallow pit materialized. He forgot to be surprised: In the pit lay Helena.

Only afterwards did everything become clear. Helena had taken her mother's suggestion to dig herself a grave literally. After everyone was asleep she'd taken a shovel, gone into the orchard where her father had hanged himself, and dug a grave. Then she'd lain down in it and swallowed half a bottle of iodine. As it happened, everyone had been in a deep sleep that night, even the dogs in the kennel.

Dr. Yaretzky thrust his finger down Helena's windpipe, forced her to retch. He roused her mother and the servants, poured half a pitcher of milk down Helena's throat. The widow embraced Dr. Yaretzky, attempting to kiss him. The court echoed with loud voices, barking, cries. Helena's tongue was burned from the poison, her hair matted with mud and clay. She was barefoot and in her nightgown. Dr. Yaretzky carried her into her room and put her to bed.

The widow tried to keep the incident secret but the town learned all about it. Dr. Yaretzky had asked Helena for her hand. Before the widow and the servants he'd kissed Helena's seared lips. She'd raised her lids, taken Yaretzky's hand, put it to her mouth, and for the second time that day—kissed it.

VII
BETWEEN YES AND NO

The town prepared itself for a splendid wedding. At the estate tailors sewed Helena's trousseau, seamstresses embroidered lingerie. The town merchants imported numerous items from Lublin and Warsaw to supplement the bride's outfit. The orchestra tuned up its instruments. A ball was scheduled at the Military Club in honor of the engaged couple. Dr. Yaretzky, however, knew no peace. He felt as if he were at the edge of disaster. Precisely at one o'clock every night he would awaken with the sensation that someone was blowing into his ear. He would sit up trembling, sweating—heavyhearted. "What am I doing?" he would ask himself. "How have I managed to ensnare myself? Why am I suddenly getting married?"

The ardor that he'd felt towards Helena the night he'd found her poisoned, had deserted him. Only apprehension remained. He was well aware of the pitfalls of married life. "Have I lost my senses?" he wondered, "have I been bewitched? But there is no such thing as black magic!"

Dr. Yaretzky recalled how he had stared through the rabbi's window. "Could the scene between the rabbi and his wife actually have unbalanced me, deprived me of my convictions, my resolutions? If so, I have no character at all!" he said aloud.

He would get up and wander like a sleepwalker from room to room in the dark. Various remedies occurred to him: To run away while there was still time; perhaps put a bullet through his brain . . . or write Helena a note breaking the engagement. He could not forget Schopenhauer's description of woman: That narrow-waisted, high-breasted, wide-hipped vessel of sex, which blind will has formed for its own purposes—to perpetuate the eternal suffering and tedium. "No! I won't do it!" he would shout. "I won't stumble into a ditch like some blind horse! Yes, I made a promise—but what is a promise? What is honor?" Yaretzky knew Schopenhauer's essay on dueling and his whole concept of honor. It was waste, refuse—a relic of the days of knighthood, an absurd anachronism! "A curse on the whole damned thing!" Yaretzky would say to himself.

After considerable struggle with himself, Dr. Yaretzky decided to run away. What ties did he have in this God-forsaken hole? Neither friends nor relatives, a house which was not his own, furniture not worth a kopeck. His money was hidden in a secret place, he could hitch up his britzska in the middle of the night, load it with clothes, books, and instruments—and be gone. What code ordained that a man must endure the human comedy to the end? No one could force him to swear faithfulness to a wife, to raise sons and daughters, to blend his seed with the seed of those who served blind will like slaves, celebrated its weddings, wailed at its funerals, grew old, broken, crushed, forgotton. It was true that he felt compassion for Helena; he agreed with Schopenhauer—pity was the basis of morality; but what of the generations he and Helena would spawn? It was worse for them. Their anguish would persist eternally. How does it go: The luckiest child is the one not born?

He had little time left, he'd have to move quickly. His maid was deaf and mute and in addition, a heavy sleeper. His coachman spent his nights with a sweetheart in a nearby village. The only obstacle was the dog. He would bark and raise a rumpus. "I'll have to give him something!" Dr. Yaretzky decided. He had various poisons in his cabinet. Would it matter whether he lived twelve years—or nine? Death was unavoidable. It was everywhere—in the bed of a woman in labor, in a child's cradle, it trailed life like a shadow. Those who are familiar with death smell the stench of shrouds even in the diapers of an infant.

When Dr. Yaretzky finally arrived at his decision it was too late. A gray dawn had appeared. Dew was on the orchard grass but he sat in it. He did not believe in colds. He leaned against the trunk of an apple tree and inhaled the aromas of dawn. He felt ravaged by the struggle that had gone on within him for almost two weeks. Insufficient sleep, inner doubt and lack of food had exhausted him. His body felt hollow inside, his skull seemed stuffed with sand. He was Dr. Yaretzky, yet, he was not Yaretzky at all. He fought alien, mysterious forces, listening as they met for the final battle, the outcome of which he could not determine until the last second. But the powers that said, "No," were nevertheless the stronger. They marshaled their arguments like armies, dispatched them to the most strategic positions, overwhelmed the affirmative faction, throttled it, pelted it with logic, mockery, blasphemy.

Dr. Yaretzky looked up at the sky. The stars shone against the dawn, divinely luminous, filled with unearthly joy. The heavenly spheres appeared festive. But was it truly so? —No, it was a deception. If there was life on other planets, it was the same pattern of gluttony and violence as on earth. Our planet also appeared shining and glorious if viewed from Mars or the Moon. Even the town slaughterhouse looked like a temple from the distance.

He spat at the sky but the spittle landed on his own knee.

VIII
SHADOWS OF THE PAST

The following night, Dr. Yaretzky made his escape. Three months later Helena left to take the nun's vows at the convent of Saint Ursula. Dressed entirely in black, she took a black trunk, much like a coffin. The widow died soon afterwards, reportedly of a broken heart. Her steward must have been a thief for the estate was left badly in debt and quickly deteriorated. Some of the property was divided among the peasants; the house was abandoned. Everyone knows that an unoccupied house quickly goes to ruin. Moss and nests covered the roof, the walls sprouted mold and toadstools, an owl perched on the chimney and hooted in the night as if mourning an old misery.

Time passed. The town now had a new doctor, a new rabbi. The new rabbi was not a sage like the other but he persevered assiduously. After the evening services he went directly to bed. At midnight, he was in his study poring over the holy books. He also wrote interpretations of the Talmud.

Fourteen years had gone by. One midnight, the rabbi raised his eyes from his book and saw someone looking into his window—a swarthy individual with black eyes, a high forehead and black mustache. At first the rabbi thought his wife had forgotten to close the shutter and some gentile was spying on him, but suddenly he realized that the shutter was indeed closed. In the pane, along with the lamp, the table and the samovar, the face was reflected. Terrified, the rabbi's cry for help choked in his throat. After a while he rose and with trembling knees went to his wife in the bedroom.

Since there is a measure of doubt even in the most pious, the rabbi himself decided that he had only fancied what he had seen and he told no one of the incident. In the morning, he ordered the scribe to examine the *Mezuzah* and that night, as a good luck charm, he placed a volume of the Zohar and a prayer shawl with phylacteries on the table. He was determined never to interrupt his prayers or look up at the window again. Deeply engrossed in his writing, having forgotten his fear, he suddenly looked up and saw the face again in the window, real and yet unreal, insubstantial, not of the world. The rabbi cried out and fainted. Hearing the thud of his body, his wife let out a mournful wail.

They revived the rabbi but he no longer could nor would deny what he had seen. He sent the beadle to summon the elders of the community, and secretly recounted his experience. After long discussion and much supposition, it was decided that three of the men would sit up with the rabbi to observe.

The first night, the three guardians sat until sunrise and saw nothing. Sensing he was suspected of fabrication and hallucinations, the rabbi swore that he had seen either a phantom or the devil. The next night the three men again kept the vigil. When the roosters had crowed and no one had appeared at the window, two of the citizens stretched out on the benches to sleep. Only one remained awake, leafing through a copy of the Mishnah. Suddenly he leaped from his seat. The rabbi, who'd been working on one of his tracts, was so startled that he overturned the inkhorn. He, himself, had seen nothing, but the other man told, with a tremor in his voice, of having seen the image in the window and furthermore, that he had recognized the face as Dr. Yaretzky's.

The other two men were astounded. Why, of all people, would Dr. Yaretzky's ghost manifest itself here? Why should the spirit of such a rogue linger at the rabbi's window?

Although the elders promised to keep the story secret, it soon became common knowledge. The rabbi was unable to continue his studies—he was constantly attended by guardians—and each time, Dr. Yaretzky revealed himself to another witness. At times he materialized within one second and immediately afterwards dissolved. Other times he lingered a moment or two. Often the upper part of his clothing was likewise visible: a thin blouse, an opened collar, a sash around his waist. He would appear in the window like a portrait in a frame, absorbed, lost in meditation, the widely opened eyes focused on one point.

Within a short time, Dr. Yaretzky began to appear in other places. One night when a peasant awoke and went to see about his horse, which, tethered, grazed in the pasture outside, he saw the figure of a man bending over the grass holding his hands as if he were lifting some weight. The peasant thought the man a thief or a gypsy and he advanced, brandishing his whip, but at that moment, the other vanished as if the earth had swallowed him. According to the peasant's description it was evident that it was the spirit of Dr. Yaretzky. The invisible something which he'd been supposedly lifting must have been Helena since an old woman swore that it was the exact spot where Helena had dug the grave after she'd swallowed the poison, and it was from there that Dr. Yaretzky had carried her into the house.

Another time, the present doctor (who'd moved into Yaretzky's old residence) was preparing to ride off in the middle of the night to visit a dying patient. His coachman went out to the stall to hitch up the britzska, and spied someone sitting in the orchard under an apple tree, his head leaning against the tree-trunk, his legs drawn up, a strange dog at his side. He was, to all appearances, asleep. The coachman was puzzled. The man did not look like a vagrant who slept under open skies, but like a gentleman. "He's probably drunk!" the coachman said to himself. He walked over to wake the other, but in that moment the figure disintegrated. Neither was there a trace left of the dog. From sheer terror the coachman began to hiccup and kept on hiccupping for three days. Only after the attack subsided was he able to tell what he'd seen.

The town separated into two camps. The faithful believed that the soul of Dr. Yaretzky wandered through all the tortures of hell and could find no resting place. The wordly citizens on the other hand, maintained that since there was no such thing as a soul, the entire thing was simply hysteria and superstition. The priest wrote a letter to the convent of Saint Ursula and an answer came back stating that Sister Helena had passed away. Dr. Yaretzky was apparently no longer alive either, since the spirits of living people do not roam about in the night. One thing remained a topic of discussion even among the believers: Why would the soul of Dr. Yaretzky hover in the window of the rabbi's study? Why should a Christian heretic seek the house of a rabbi?

Soon there was talk that lights could be seen at night in the windows of the crumbling estate. An old crone who walked past the ruin swore that she'd heard a thin voice as if that of a mother crooning lullabies to her infant and the old woman had recognized it as Helena's voice. Another woman confirmed this and added that on moonlit nights one could see on the wall of Helena's room, the shadow of a crib. . . .

After a while the ruin was demolished and a granery erected on the site. The rabbi's house was rebuilt. The doctor added a wing to his house and ordered the apple trees chopped down. Heaven and earth conspire that everything which has been, be rooted out and reduced to dust. Only the dreamers, who dream while awake, call back the shadows of the past and braid from unspun threads—unwoven nets.

Translated by
Elaine Gottlieb and
June Ruth Flaum

Shiddah and Kuziba

I

Shiddah and her child, Kuziba, a schoolboy, were sitting nine yards inside the earth at a place where two ledges of rock came together and an underground stream was flowing. Shiddah's body was made of cobwebs; her hair reached to her anklebones; her feet were like those of a chicken; and she had the wings of a bat. Kuziba, who looked like his mother, had, in addition, donkey ears and wax horns. Kuziba was sick with a high fever. Every half hour his mother gave him medicine made of devil's dung mixed with copper juice, the darkness of a ditch, and the droppings of a red crow. Shiddah, leaning over her son, licked his navel with her long tongue. Kuziba was sleeping the restless sleep of the sick. Suddenly the boy woke up.

"I'm frightened, mother," he said.

"Of what, dear?"

"Of light. Of human beings."

Shiddah trembled; and then spat on her son to ward off such evils.

"What are you talking about, child? We're safe here—far from light and far from human beings. It's as dark as Egypt here, thank God, and as silent as a cemetery. We're protected by nine yards of solid rock."

"But they say men can break rocks," said the boy.

"Old wives' tales!" countered his mother. "The power of man is only on the surface. The heights are for angels. The depths are for us. The lot of man is to creep on the skin of the earth like a louse."

"But what *are* human beings, mother? Tell me."

"What are they? They're the waste of creation, offal; where sin is brewed in a kettle, mankind is the foam. Man is the mistake of God."

"How can God the Almighty make a mistake?" asked Kuziba.

"That is a secret, my child," answered Shiddah. "For when God created the last of all the worlds, the earth, his love for our mistress, Lilith, was stronger than ever. Only for an instant his gaze wandered, and in that instant he produced man—an evil mixture of flesh, love, dung, and lust.

"Man!" Shiddah spat. "He has a white skin but inside he is red. He shouts as if he were strong, but really he is weak and shaky. Throw a stone and he breaks; use a thong and he bleeds. In heat he melts. In cold he freezes. There is a bellows in his chest which has to contract and expand constantly. In his left side is a small sac which must throb and quiver all the time. He stuffs himself with mildew of a kind which grows in mud or sand. This mildew he has to swallow constantly and after it passes through his body he must drop it out. He depends on a thousand accidents, and that's why he is so nasty and angry."

"But what do human beings do, mother?"

"Evil," Shiddah answered her son, "only evil. But that keeps them busy so that they leave us in peace. Why, some of them even deny our existence. They think life can only breed on the surface of the earth. Like all fools they consider themselves clever.

"Imagine! They study wisdom on crushed wood pulp smeared with blotches of ink. And their ideas come from a slimy matter which they carry in a bony skull on their necks. They can't even run the way animals can: their legs are too feeble. But one thing they do possess in great measure: insolence. If God the Omnipotent did not have so much patience he would have destroyed such rabble long ago."

Kuziba, who had listened intently to his mother's words, was not reassured. He stared at his mother feverishly.

"I'm afraid of them, mother. I'm afraid."

"Don't be, Kuziba. They can't come here."

"In my sleep I dream about them." Kuziba trembled.

"Don't shake so, my darling little devil." Shiddah caressed her son. "Dreams are silly. They too come from the surface where chaos rules."

II

Kuziba, who had lain for some time in a deep sleep, suddenly cried out. His mother awakened him.

"What's the matter, my son?"

"I'm frightened."

"Again?"

"I was dreaming about a man."

"What did he look like, my child?"

"So fierce. He made a noise that almost made me go deaf. And he had a light that was blinding me. I would have died from fear if you hadn't waked me."

"Be still, my son. I will chant a spell for you."

And Shiddah murmured:

Lord of the Depths
Curse the evil surface.
Lord of all Silence
Destroy the Din.

Save us great Father
From Light, from Words,
From Man his Deceit.
Save us, Lord God.

For a while it was quiet. Kuziba dozed off. Shiddah cradled her only son, swaying rhythmically above him. She thought of her husband, Hurmiz, who did not live at home. He went to the Yeshivah of Chittim and Tachtim which was thousands of yards deeper, nearer the center of the earth. There he studied the secret of silence. Because silence has many degrees. As Shiddah knew, no matter how quiet it is, it can be even quieter. Silence is like fruits which have pits within pits, seeds within seeds. There is a final silence, a last point so small that it is nothing, yet so mighty that worlds can be created from it. This last point is the essence of all essences. Everything else is external, nothing but skin, peel, surface. He who has reached the final point, the last degree of silence, knows nothing of time and space, of death and lust. There male and female are forever united; will and deed are the same. This last silence is God. But God himself keeps on penetrating deeper into Himself. He descends into his depths. His nature is like a cave without bottom. He keeps on investigating his own abyss.

Kuziba had fallen asleep. Shiddah, too, rested her head against a stone pillow. She imagined dreamily how Kuziba would grow up and become a big devil; how he would marry and become a father, and how she, Shiddah, would serve her daughter-in-law and her grandchildren. The babies would begin to call her grandma; and she would delouse their heads. She would braid the girls' hair, clean the boys' noses, take them to *Cheder*, feed them, put them to sleep. Then the grandchildren themselves would grow up and be led under black canopies to marry the sons and daughters of the most reputable and well-established demons.

Her husband, Hurmiz, would become a rabbi of the netherworld, giving out amulets, reciting incantations. He would teach imps the chapter of curses on Mount Ebal, and the curses which Balaam should have used on the Israelites; he would teach them the prophecies of the false prophets, the words of temptation which the primeval snake used in the Garden of Eden; he would teach them the cunning of the fallen angels, the confusion of tongues of those who built the tower of Babel; he would instruct them in the perversities of men at the time of the flood, in the vanities of Jeroboam and Ahab, Jezebel and Vashti. Then Hurmiz would become King of the Demons. He would be offered the throne in the Abyss of the Great Female, a thousand miles away from the surface where no one had ever heard of man and his insanity.

Suddenly Shiddah's daydreaming was interrupted. There was a terrible thundering. Shiddah leapt to her feet. A racketing clamor filled the cave as if a thousand hammers were beating. Everything shook. Kuziba woke up with a scream.

"Mother, mother," yelled the boy. "Run, run."

"Help, demons! Help!" Shiddah shouted.

She caught up Kuziba in her arms and tried to flee. But where to? From all sides came a rumbling and cracking. Rocks were crashing down; stones were flying about. The narrow hole which led further underground to the homes of the richer demons was already clogged. A rain of dust, sparks, stone splinters struck the mother and son. Then a light, awful, glaring, a thing with no name in the netherworld, blinded them with its approach. Presently, a monstrous, spiraling machine plunged through the ledge of rock in front of them. Shiddah fell back to the opposite wall, but at that moment it too shattered into a thousand pieces. A second light appeared and another gigantic screw, twisting round and round, pushing with a strange and overwhelming power, ready to crush and grind everything with a cruelty beyond good and evil, broke into their home.

Kuziba, with a terrible sigh, fainted. He hung in Shiddah's arms as if he were dead. Shiddah saw a crevice among some stones and crawled in. She huddled there stiff with fear. What she saw was more horrible than all the horror stories she had ever heard from all the old grandmothers and great-grandmothers. The drills turned a last time and then were silent. The stones stopped falling and in the smoke and dust men appeared—tall, two-legged, dirty, stinking, with white teeth in faces black with tar, and with eyes from which glared iniquity, malice, and pride. They spoke an ugly gibberish; laughed with abandonment; danced; stretched out their paws to one another. Then they began to drink a poisonous beverage, the sheer smell of which made Shiddah faint. She wanted to rouse Kuziba, but she was afraid, if he came to, he would begin screaming, or even might die at the sight of such monsters. The only thing Shiddah could do now was pray. She prayed to Satan, to Asmodeus, to Lilith, and to all the other powers which maintain creation. Help us, she called from the cranny in which she was hiding, help us, not because of my merit but because of the merit of my scholarly husband, because of my innocent child and my worthy ancestors. Long, long, Shiddah knelt in the crack in the stones and prayed and wept. When she again opened her eyes, the ugly images had gone and the noise had subsided. What remained was garbage, a stench, and a ball of light which hung above her head like fire from Gehenna. Only now did she wake up her son.

"Kuziba, Kuziba. Wake up!" Shiddah called to her son. "We are in great danger!"

Kuziba opened his eyes.

"What is this? Oh mother. Light!"

The boy trembled and screamed. For a long while Shiddah comforted him, kissing him and caressing him. But they could not stay there any more. They had to find refuge. But where? The road down to Hurmiz was cut off. Shiddah was now a grass widow, Kuziba a fatherless child. There was only one way to go. Shiddah had heard the saying that if you cannot go down you have to go up. Mother and son began to climb to the surface. Up there, there would also be caves, marshes, graves, dark rocky crevices; there too, she had heard, there were dense forests and empty deserts. Man had not covered the whole surface with his greed. There, too, lived demons, imps, shades, hobgoblins. True, they were refugees, exiles from the netherworld. But still, exile is better than slavery.

For Shiddah knew that the last victory would be to darkness. Until then, demons who were forsaken or driven-out would have to suffer patience. But a time would come when the light of the Universe would be extinguished. All the stars would be snuffed out; all voices, silenced; all surfaces, cut off.

God and Satan would be one. The remembrance of man and his abominations would be nothing but a bad dream which God had spun out for a while to distract himself in his eternal night.

Translated by Elizabeth Pollet

Caricature

The walls of the study where Dr. Boris Margolis sat reading his manuscript were lined with books and on the floor and sofa was a litter of newspapers, magazines, discarded envelopes. In addition, there were two wastepaper baskets crammed with papers which the doctor had forbidden anyone to discard until he had one more look at them. Books, their pages still uncut, manuscripts, his own as well as other people's, letters which remained unopened, had become a curse in the apartment. They were dust collectors; bugs were to be seen crawling on them. The smell of print, sealing wax, cigar smoke, was omnipresent in the place, an acrid and musty odor. Every day Dr. Margolis argued with his wife, Mathilda, about cleaning the room but the ash trays remained filled with cigar butts and pieces of food. Mathilda kept him on a diet and hunger was forever assaulting the doctor. He was constantly nibbling egg-cookies, halva, chocolate; he also liked a taste of brandy. He had been warned about scattering ashes, but, nevertheless, there were small gray heaps on the window sill and armchairs. The doctor had ordered that no window be opened; the wind might blow his papers away. Nothing could be discarded without his agreement and Dr. Margolis never agreed. He would peer at the paper in question from beneath his bushy eyebrows and plead, "No, I'd better keep this around just a little bit longer."

"How much longer is that?" Mathilda would ask. "Until the coming of the Messiah?"

"Indeed, how much longer?" Dr. Margolis would say with a sniff. When you are sixty-nine years old and have a weak heart, you can't postpone things forever. He had taken on so many obligations the day was too short. Scholars kept writing to him here in Warsaw from England and America, even from Germany where that maniac Hitler had come to power. Since Dr. Margolis published criticism in an academic journal from time to time, authors sent him their books to review. He had once subscribed to several philosophical magazines and, though he had long since given up renewing his subscriptions, the issues continued to arrive along with demands for payment. Most of the scholars of his generation had died. He himself, for a while, had been as good as forgotten. But the new generation had rediscovered him, and he was now showered with letters of praise as well as all sorts of requests. Just when he had at last resigned himself to never seeing his masterpiece in print (the work had been the labor of twenty-five years), a Swiss publisher had got in touch with him. He had gone as far as to give Dr. Margolis a five hundred franc advance. But now that the publisher was waiting for the manuscript, the realization had come to Dr. Margolis that the work was full of mistakes and inaccuracies, even contradictions. He was uncertain whether his philosophy, a return to metaphysics, had any value. At sixty-nine he no longer had the need to see his name in print. If he could not bring out a consistent system, it was better to keep silent.

Now Dr. Margolis sat, small, broad-shouldered, his head bent forward, his white hair blowing about his head like foam. His goatee pointed upward and to the side of his gray moustache, singed from the cigars he had smoked down to the butt, his cheeks hung limp. Between the thick, bushy eyebrows and the pouchlike bags underlining the eyes, were the eyes themselves, dark, and despite their keen, penetrating gaze, good-natured. The retinas were covered with brown, hornlike specks; cataracts had begun to form and sooner or later the doctor would have to undergo an operation. A small beard sprouted from the doctor's nose and wisps of hair protruded from his ears. Every morning Mathilda reminded him to put on a dressing gown and slippers, but as soon as he arose, he dressed in his black suit, his spats and a stiff collar and black tie. He heeded neither his wife nor his doctors. He poured the medicines which had been prescribed down the drain, threw away the pills, smoked continually, consumed every variety of sweet and fatty foods. Now he sat reading and grimacing. He pulled at his beard, sniffed and grunted.

"Rubbish. Tripe. Just no good."

Mathilda appeared at the door, small and round as a barrel, wearing a silk kimono and open sandals which left her twisted toes exposed. Whenever Dr. Margolis looked at her, he was astonished. Was this really the woman he had fallen in love with and taken from another man thirty-two years ago? She had grown smaller and smaller and puffier and puffier; her stomach stuck out like a man's. Since she had practically no neck, her large square head just sat on her shoulders. Her nose was flat and her thick lips and jowls made him think of a bulldog. Her scalp showed through her hair. Worst of all she had begun to grow a beard, and though she had tried to cut, shave, singe off the hair, it had merely grown denser. The skin of her face was covered with roots from each of which sprouted a few prickly shoots of a nondescript color. Rouge peeled from the creases on her face like plaster. Her eyes stared with a masculine severity. Dr. Margolis remembered a saying of Schopenhauer: Woman has the appearance and mentality of a child. If she becomes intellectually mature, she develops the face of a man.

"What do you want, eh?" Dr. Margolis asked.

"Open a window. It stinks in here."

"All right, let it stink."

"What about the manuscript? They're waiting for it in Berne."

"Let them wait."

"How long are they supposed to wait? Such opportunities don't come every day."

Dr. Margolis laid down his pen. He half-turned towards Mathilda and blew a cloud of smoke at her. He took a last pull and spat out a small fragment of tobacco which was still smoldering.

"I'll send back the five hundred francs, Mathilda."

Mathilda edged away.

"Send back the money? You're mad."

"It's no use. I can't publish something I don't even like. It doesn't matter if others tear me to pieces. But I must be convinced the work has merit."

"All these years you've insisted it's a work of genius."

"I said no such thing. I hoped it might be worth something but at home they used to say: Hoping and having are worlds apart." Dr. Margolis groped for another cigar.

"I won't return one franc," Mathilda cried.

"Come now, do you want me to become a thief in my old age?"

"Send them the manuscript then. It's the best thing you've done. What crazy idea has got into you? And anyway, how can you be your own judge?"

"Who can, then? You?"

"Yes, I. Other people publish a book a year, but you brood over your wretched scribblings like a hen over her eggs. . . . You fiddle around and spoil everything. . . . I don't have the money; I've spent it. . . . The less you tinker with it, the better off you'll be. I'm beginning to think you're getting senile."

"Maybe—maybe I am."

"I don't have the money any longer."

"Well, well, it'll be all right," Dr. Margolis grunted half to Mathilda and half to himself. For days he had been preparing to tell her his decision, but he had feared a scene. Now the worst was over. One way or another he'd manage to dig up the five hundred francs. If everything else failed, he'd borrow from a bank. Morris Traybitcher would sign for him. And as for his so-called immortality, that was lost anyway. He had squandered his last years (the years in Berlin as well as those in Warsaw) on lectures and articles and Zionist conferences. And indeed what if the work were published and several professors praised it? Now philosophy had become nothing but the history of human illusions. Hume had given it the *coup de grace* and had buried it. Kant's attempts at resurrection had failed. Those who had followed the German had written merely afterthoughts. With his tobacco-stained fingers Dr. Margolis began to search for a match. He had an overpowering desire to smoke. Then once more he turned toward the door.

"Still here, eh?"

"I just want you to know that I intend to send the manuscript tomorrow whether you like it or not."

"So you're in command now? No, today it goes out with the garbage."

"You wouldn't dare. What will we do in our our old age? Go begging?"

Dr. Margolis grinned.

"Our old age is already here. Do you think we'll live as long as Methuselah?"

"I don't expect to die just yet."

"All right, all right, close the door and leave me in peace. Just don't interfere in my affairs."

He heard the door slam, found his matches and lit a cigar. He inhaled the bitter smoke deeply and read three more sentences which he also disliked. The very last statement he couldn't even recognize as his. If it hadn't been in his handwriting, he would have assumed someone else had written it. It sounded trite. The syntax was faulty. The words had no relevance to what was under discussion. Dr. Margolis sat with his mouth open. Had it been a *dybbuk* who was responsible? He began to shake his head as though there was something supernatural involved. He recalled a sentence from Ecclesiastes: "And further, by these, my son, be admonished: of making books there is no end." Evidently even then there had been too much scribbling. He remembered the bottle of cognac in his bookcase.

"I think I'll have a sip. At this point it can't do me any harm."

Days passed and Dr. Margolis could not decide what to do. The more he worked on the manuscript, the more confused he became. It had some good ideas in it, but the structure was poor and there was a general limpness to the work. He tried cutting, but there was no cohesion to the paragraphs he kept. The book should be entirely rewritten, but he no longer had the required energy. Recently his hands had begun to tremble. His pen skipped and blotted; he omitted letters and words. He even found misspellings and apparently he had forgotten German. Occasionally he caught himself using Yiddish idioms. What was more, he had developed the habit of dozing off as soon as he sat down to work. At night he would lie awake for hours, his brain strangely alert. He would make imaginary speeches, think up strange puns, and argue with such celebrities as Wundt, Kuno Fischer and Professor Bauch. But during the day he tired quickly. His shoulders would sag and his head would nod. He would dream he was in Switzerland—penniless, hungry, homeless, about to be deported by the authorities. "Perhaps, Mathilda is right after all and I am getting senile," Dr. Margolis said to himself. "The brain is indeed a machine and it does wear out. Possibly the materialists are correct after all." The perverse thought crossed his mind. In a world where everything was topsy-turvy, Feuerbach might even be the Messiah.

That evening Dr. Margolis went to a meeting. It concerned a Hebrew encyclopedia which had been begun years before in Berlin. Now that Hitler had become Chancellor, the editorial board had moved to Warsaw. The truth was that the entire undertaking was absurd. Neither the funds nor the contributors were available. In addition, Hebrew still lacked the technical terminology for a modern encyclopedia. But the board would not give up the plan. They had found a rich patron willing to contribute money. And so a few refugees supported themselves through the enterprise. Well, it was all just a question of sponging, Dr. Margolis remarked to himself. . . . But, nevertheless, there could be no harm in spending a few hours in such a gathering. The meeting was to be held in the donor's house and Dr. Margolis traveled there by taxi. He rode upstairs in a paneled elevator, and once inside he found himself seated at the head of the table. The host, Morris Traybitcher, a small man with a bald head, pink cheeks, and a pointed belly, introduced him first to his giant of a wife and then to his daughters, bleached blondes in dresses with low necklines. Dr. Margolis conversed with the wife and daughters in broken Polish. Tea, jam, pastries, liqueurs were served and, though Dr. Margolis had already had his dinner, these delicacies stimulated his appetite. He smoked his wealthy host's Havana cigars, ate, drank, meanwhile trying to clarify the difficulties involved in publishing such an encyclopedia.

"Forgetting the other problems for a moment, there's Hitler himself who isn't going to stay in Berchtesgaden. One of these days he'll be on his way here. . . ."

"You may have to eat your words, Dr. Margolis," Traybitcher said, interrupting him.

"Spengler was right. Europe is committing suicide."

"We survived Haman and we'll also survive Hitler."

"May it be so. Jews build everything on their faith in survival, but what is the basis of that faith? Oh, let's go ahead and publish the encyclopedia. It won't kill any children."

Of those present some spoke Yiddish, and others a kind of German. One man who had a short white beard and gold-rimmed glasses spoke in Hebrew with a Sephardic accent. There was also a refugee professor from Berlin who wore a monocle in his left eye and looked like a Junker. He bore himself more stiffly than any Prussian Dr. Margolis had ever met and alluded to the *Ost-Juden.* Dr. Margolis listened with only half an ear. Each of these calculating individuals had his ambitions and his idiosyncrasies. They were after the few zlotys and the tiny bit of prestige the encyclopedia offered. The philanthropist went as far as to suggest that the work be named after him: The Traybitcher Encyclopedia. Yet he had only contributed a negligible part of the expenses. Microbes, Dr. Margolis thought, nothing but microbes. A glob of matter, a breath of spirit. The whole business lasted but an instant, as the prayer book said. Ah, but the rent must be paid and when money was lacking, life could be very bitter. The forces that had created man hadn't stinted on suffering. . . . It was getting late, and Morris Traybitcher began to yawn. As usual, the decision was to call another meeting. The guests took their leave, each kissing their hostess' heavy braceleted hands. The elevator was so crowded Dr. Margolis tried to pull in his stomach, and when they arrived at the courtyard, they found the gate locked. The janitor growled at them; a dog barked. Dr. Margolis looked about for a cab, but couldn't find one. The professor from Berlin was becoming impatient.

"Ach," he said, "Warsaw is nothing but an Asiatic town."

But finally a cab did stop for him and he drove away. Dr. Margolis waited so long that he gave up and went in search of a streetcar. He felt bloated, could hardly see in the badly lit street, and went tapping his cane before him like a blind man. At first it seemed that he was sliding downhill, and then he got the impression that it was the sidewalk that was slanting. He sought to find out from a passerby in which direction to go, but the man didn't answer. —I'm going to catch it from Mathilda, he thought. She never stopped preaching to him about the necessity of going to bed early. He began to meditate about her. In the old days she had never interfered in his affairs. She had had her home and her clothes and her spas where she went to drink mineral water. When he attempted to speak to her about philosophy, she had refused to listen; nor had she read the reviews of his work he had showed her. She had avoided everything intellectual. Now that he had lost his ambition, she had become ambitious for him. She read his early writings, and whenever they were invited out, she called him professor, praised him, even sought to explain his philosophy. She repeated his jokes, maligned his enemies, took over his mannerisms. He was shamed by her ignorance and her exaggerated loyalty. Yet none of this prevented her from scolding him at home in the coarsest language. As the Polish proverb says: Old age is no joy. No, old age was merely a parody of one's youth.

Finally, Dr. Margolis found the proper streetcar and rode home. He had to wait interminably for the janitor to open the gate. Panting heavily, he mounted the dark steps and then stopped to rest. His heart pounded, every now and again missed a beat. There was a tugging sensation at his knees as if he were climbing a mountain. He could hear his breath coming in snorts. He wiped the sweat from his brow, unlocked the door, and entered on tiptoes so as not to awake Mathilda. He took off his clothes in the living room leaving only his underpants on. The mirror reflected his unclothed body—his chest covered with white hair, his bulging stomach, his excessively short legs and his yellow toenails. Thank the Lord we don't go around naked, Dr. Margolis meditated. No animal was as ugly as homo sapiens. . . . He walked into the bedroom and saw in the semi-darkness that Mathilda's bed was empty. This frightened him and he switched on the light.

"What kind of nonsense is this?" Dr. Margolis asked out loud. "She can't have thrown herself out of the window?" He went back to the hall and noticed a light on in his study. What could she be doing in there so late? He walked to the door and threw it open: There sat Mathilda clad in his dressing gown and slippers asleep at the desk. The manuscript lay open in front of her. A half-smoked cigar was propped against the ash tray and a bottle of cognac and a glass stood among the litter of papers. Never before had her beard seemed to him so grotesquely long and thick; it was as though during the few hours he had been absent it had been growing wildly. Her head was almost bald. She was snoring heavily. In sleep her eyebrows were drawn together, and her hairy, masculine nose protruded; her nostrils were clotted with small tufts of hair. In some mysterious way she had grown to resemble him—she was like the image he had just seen in the mirror. Man and wife share a pillow so long that their heads grow alike, Dr. Margolis quoted to himself, recalling the proverb. But, no, there was more to it than that. This was a biological imitation, like those creatures that simulate being trees and bushes or the bird whose bill looks like a banana. But what was the purpose of this imitation in old age? How could it benefit the species? He felt both compassion and disgust. Evidently she wished to convince herself that the book was worth publishing. On her tightly shut lids was stamped disappointment, the look of disillusionment that sometimes lingers on the face of a corpse. He started to wake her:

"Mathilda. Mathilda."

She stirred, then awoke and rose to her feet. Man and wife viewed each other, silent and amazed, with that strangeness which sometimes follows a life of intimacy. Dr. Margolis wanted to scold her, but he could not. It wasn't her fault. This was apparently the last stage of declining femininity.

"Come to sleep," he said. "It's late, you ninny."

Mathilda shook herself and pointed to the manuscript. "It's a great book, a work of genius."

Translated by
Shulamith Charney and
Cecil Hemley

The Beggar Said So

I

One hot summer day a big wagon, drawn by one horse, lumbered into the market place of Yanov. It was piled high with motley rags and bedding, laden with cans and buckets, and from the axle between the rear wheels a lantern hung. On top of everything a flower pot and a cage with a little yellow bird swayed precariously. The driver of the wagon was dark, with a pitch-black beard. He wore a cap with a leather visor and a coat not cut in the usual style. At first glance one could have taken him for an ordinary Russian. But the woman with him wore on her head the familiar Jewish coif. Jews, then, after all. Instantly, from all the little shops round about, the Jews of the town rushed out to meet the new arrivals. The stranger stood there in the market place with his whip in his hand.

"Wher-r-re's your magistr-r-rate?" he demanded. He pronounced his "r's" in the dialect of Great Poland, hard and sharp.

"And what would you need the magistrate for?"

"I want to be a chimney sweep," said the newcomer.

"And why should a Jew want to be a chimney sweep?"

"I served in the Army for twenty-five years. I have my working papers."

"There's a chimney sweep in town already."

"But the beggar said there wasn't," the newcomer insisted.

"What beggar?"

"Why, the one that came to our town."

It seemed that the man—his name was Moshe—had been a chimney sweep in some small town on the other side of the river Vistula, not far from the Prussian border. One day a beggar who traveled from place to place had come to that town and had said something about a chimney sweep being needed in Yanov. Moshe and his wife had lost no time; they had loaded all their worldly goods onto a wagon and set out for Yanov.

The young men watching them smiled, nudged each other and exchanged meaningful glances. The older householders shrugged their shoulders.

"Why didn't you write a letter first?" they asked Moshe.

"I can't w-r-rite," was the answer.

"So you can get someone else to write for you. Beggars have made up stories before."

"But the beggar said. . . ."

All talk and counter-arguments proved vain. To every question the man had only one answer: "The beggar said so." One might have thought his wife would have had more sense, but she, too, had the same stock rejoinder: "The beggar said so." The crowd of townspeople grew swiftly and the strange tale passed from mouth to mouth. The onlookers began to whisper to each other about it; they shook their heads and made crude puns. One of the men, a flour dealer, called out:

"Just think, believing a poor tramp like that!"

"Maybe the beggar was the Prophet Elijah in disguise," jeered another.

The school children came out from the *Cheder* and mimicked the new arrivals. "The beggar said so," they hooted after them. The young girls giggled while the older women wrung their hands and lamented the lot of these poor fools from Great Poland. In the meantime Moshe the chimney sweep filled one of his cans with water at the town pump and gave his horse a drink. Then he proceeded to fasten a bag of oats around the animal's jaws. From the horse's collar which was studded with bits of brass two pine branches protruded stiffly. The shaft was painted blue. Everyone soon saw that the two travelers had with them, besides the horse and the bird, an odd assortment of geese, ducks, chickens, and one black rooster with a red comb—all in one big cage.

In Yanov at the time there were no vacant dwellings; temporarily, therefore, the two strangers were put up at the poorhouse. A coachman took their horse into his own stable, and someone else bought the fowl. Moshe's spouse, Mindel, immediately joined the other *shnorrers'* wives in the kitchen of the poorhouse where she cooked some porridge. Moshe, himself, went off to the study house to recite a few chapters from the Book of Psalms. And a new byword became fashionable in Yanov: "But the beggar said so." The schoolboys never tired of questioning Moshe and of laughing up their sleeves.

"Tell us," they would query, "just what did he look like, that beggar?"

"Like all other beggars," Moshe would reply.

"What kind of a beard did he have?"

"Yellow."

"Don't you know that men who grow yellow hair are cheaters?"

"How should I know?" Moshe would report. "I'm a simple man. The beggar said so, and I believed him."

"If he had told you that the rabbi's wife lays eggs, would you have believed that too?"

Moshe did not answer. He was a man well into his fifties, though still without one grey hair. His face was tanned like that of a gypsy. His back was straight; his shoulders and chest, broad. He produced for the school teacher's inspection two medals which he had gotten in the Tsar's service for proficiency in riding and marksmanship, and he told of his experiences as a soldier. He had been one of the young boys inducted by force. His father had been a blacksmith. He, Moshe, had still been a student at the *Cheder* when a child-snatcher from the Tsar's army had taken him away. But he, Moshe, had refused to eat forbidden foods and had fasted until he was faint with hunger. The village priest had tried to convert him, but he had a *mezuzah* which his mother had given him as well as the fringed ritual garment worn next to the body to remind him of his God at all times. Yes, they had whipped him, flogged him too with wet switches, but he had not given in. He had remained a Jew. When they tortured him, he had cried out, "Hear, O Israel, the Lord our God is One."

Moshe also told about the time, years later, when he had fallen asleep while on sentry duty and his gun had slipped from his hand. If he had been caught napping, he would have been sent to Siberia. But lo, his dead grandfather had appeared to him in a dream and awakened him. He had had another close call: while crossing a frozen river, he had been stranded on an ice floe. Once too he had been attacked by a wild ox. But he had managed to grab the beast by its horns—he still bore the scar on his wrist. The Tsar's veterans had a reputation for telling tall tales, but everyone believed Moshe; it was clear from the way he told his stories that he had not made them up.

Not long after the arrival of Moshe and his wife, a room was found for them to live in and a stable for the horse. Just at that time one of the Yanov water carriers died; Moshe procured a wooden yoke and became a water carrier. His wife, Mindel, went every Thursday to knead dough in the baking troughs and, besides that job, she stripped feathers for the bedding of new brides. Gradually the two newcomers grew accustomed to Yanov. Yet one question still burrowed deep in the heart of Moshe. Why should the beggar have deceived him so? Had not he, Moshe, given his guest, the beggar, his own bed while he himself tossed about on the ground all night? Not to brag about it, but on that Sunday morning, hadn't he given his guest a loaf of bread and a slab of cheese to take on the way? Why, then, should the beggar have wanted to make a fool of him? Moshe often discussed the riddle with his wife. But she did not know the answer either, and each time he broached the subject, she would say:

"Moshe, take my advice and stop thinking about it."

"But . . . why should the beggar have said so if it wasn't true?" he would persist.

Moshe knew that wandering beggars can turn up anywhere.

Every Sabbath he looked over the transients gathered at the synagogue entrance to see if this one beggar was among them. But the years passed and the beggar never came. Was the man afraid that Moshe might take revenge? Or, perhaps, Moshe thought, God had punished him and he had died on the road. In time, the odd thing was that Moshe was not even angry any longer. He had made up his mind that he would not even give the beggar a beating if he were to meet him again. He would simply take him by the neck and say:

"Why did you make a fool of me, contemptible creature?"

Several coachmen tried to persuade Moshe to sell his horse. The wells from which water was drawn for the town of Yanov were nearby so that a water carrier had no need of a horse. And why, they argued, should he have to feed an animal for nothing? But Moshe refused to part with his old mare. He and his wife were fond of animals. God had not granted them any children, but a variety of living things—stray dogs, cats, birds that could no longer fly—had joined their household. The wife would buy a live carp for the Sabbath, but instead of cleaning it and chopping it up she would let it swim about in a washtub for weeks until it finally died of natural causes. Even though one beggar had misused their kindness, these two did not take out their chagrin on other little people. Moshe's wife carried groats to the poorhouse, and every Friday night Moshe would take a wayfarer home as his guest for the Sabbath. To every one of them he would tell the story of what had happened to him and at the end he would ask, "Now why should the beggar have said so?"

II

Late one winter night, Moshe was sitting in his chair soaking his feet in a tub of water. His wife had opened the door of a little cage and a tiny yellow bird was flying about the room. They had taught it a number of tricks. For instance, Moshe would place some millet seeds between his fingers and the bird would take them. Or else he would put one single grain on his lips and the bird would snatch it with its beak, exchanging a kiss with the master.

The oven was warm and the door locked tightly against the cold outside. The woman sat in a corner darning socks. Suddenly, Moshe's head sank down on his chest; he fell asleep and at once began to dream. He dreamed that the soot in the chimney of the poorhouse had caught fire. A bright flame shot out from the chimney and was melting all the snow on the shingle roof. Moshe awoke with a start.

"Mindel," he called to his wife. "There's a fire at the poorhouse."

"How do you know?"

"I saw it in a dream."

"A dream can fool."

"No, it's true," said Moshe.

In vain did his wife argue that it was bitter outside and that he might catch cold—Heaven forbid—if he went out so soon after soaking his feet. Hurrying, Moshe put on his boots, his fur coat and his sheepskin cap. In his closet he still had his chimney sweep's broom, with the rope and iron plummet. He took them with him now as he left the house. He walked through Lublin Street and the Street of the Synagogue and then arrived at the poorhouse. There he saw everything exactly as it had been in his dream. The chimney spouted fiery sparks. The snow near it had melted. Moshe began to shout as hard as he could but the people in the poorhouse did not hear him. Indeed, even if they had waked immediately, they would hardly have been able to save themselves for all of them were old, sick and lame. There was no ladder. Moshe attempted to scale the wall. He caught hold of a giant icicle but that broke off. Then he clung to a shingle but it, too, fell from the eaves before he could climb up. Already, a part of the roof was on fire. In desperation, Moshe grabbed his broom with the iron plummet and with a forceful heave aimed it at the chimney. Amazingly, at the first try it landed in the chimney. The rope hung out; Moshe grasped it and, like an acrobat, he swung himself onto the roof. There was no water; quickly he scooped up snow and patting it into balls threw them into the chimney, all the while bellowing at the top of his voice. But no one heard him. The poorhouse was some distance away from the town; besides, the wind was howling. And the people of Yanov were sound sleepers.

When Moshe failed to return home, his wife put on her boots and padded jacket and went to the poorhouse to see what was keeping him. The dream was true: there he was, standing on the roof. The fire was out but the chimney was still smoking. Pale moonlight shone on the eery scene. By now some of the old people inside had waked and come out, carrying a scoop and shovel. They crowded around. All declared that had it not been for Moshe, the building would have burned to cinders and they would all have perished inside. What with the wind blowing in the direction of the town, the fire could have spread to the synagogue, the bathhouse, the study house and, yes, even to the houses in the market place. And then not only would the houses have been burned-out shells, but there would have been more deaths from cold and exposure.

By the next day the report of the feat of Moshe the water carrier had spread through the town. The mayor appointed a commission to inspect all the chimneys, and the investigation revealed that the town chimney sweep had not done his job in months. They found him in his room, dead drunk, with a straw in his mouth, still sipping vodka from a cask. He was sent packing and, in his place, Moshe became the official chimney sweep of the town of Yanov.

And now a marvelous thing came to pass.

A few days later, when Moshe went to the poorhouse and the inmates crowded round him to thank him and to shower him with blessings, he noticed someone whose features seemed familiar. The man's beard was a mixture of yellow and gray. He was lying on a straw sack covered with rags. The face from which the eyes bulged out was yellow with jaundice. Moshe stopped short and thought in wonder: Where have I met him before? I could swear that I know this man. And then he clasped his hands together in amazement. Why, this was none other than the beggar, the very same one who, years ago, had told him that they needed a chimney sweep in Yanov. A stream of tears gushed forth from Moshe's eyes.

Yes, it was the beggar. He had long forgotten his words but he did recall that in that year and at that time he had spent the Sabbath in that village in Great Poland. He even recalled that he had stayed with some chimney sweep there.

And what was the fruit of all this questioning, of this investigation? Why, it had become quite clear to Moshe that the whole chain of events had been directed from On High. Years ago, this one beggar had been ordained to find a man who would one day save him and all the other people of Yanov from death. It was plain, then, that this beggar had been an instrument of God. Besides, his words had come true after all. Not at the time he said them, to be sure, but much later, for now Moshe had indeed become the official chimney sweep of Yanov. The longer Moshe thought about it, the more clearly did he see the hand of Divine Providence in it all. It was beyond his grasp. Imagine! Holy angels in Heaven thinking of Moshe the Chimney Sweep and sending him messengers with prophecies, just as in the story of Father Abraham!

Moshe was overcome by awe and humility. Had the poorhouse floor not been so dirty he would have fallen upon his face right there and prostrated himself and given thanks to the Almighty. A sob came from his throat and his beard grew sodden with his tears. After he had recovered his composure, he lifted the beggar's frail body in his arms and bore him home upon his shoulders. He washed him, bathed him, dressed him in a clean shirt and laid him on his bed. Mindel immediately went to the stove and made some soup. And the people of the town who for so many years had poked fun at Moshe and had dubbed him "But-The-Beggar-Said-So" took the events to heart and told their children to stop using that name.

III

For over three months the beggar lay in Moshe's bed while Moshe slept on the floor. Gradually the poor man regained some of his strength and wanted to go on the road again, but Moshe and his wife would not hear of it. The beggar had neither wife nor child and he was much too old and weak to wander about. He remained with the pair. Regularly he went to the study house to pray and recite psalms. His eyes failed and he grew almost blind. Other wayfarers told story after story of noblemen, merchants and rabbis, but this beggar was silent. When he finished his reading of the Book of Psalms, he would immediately start all over again. He had also memorized whole passages from the Mishnah. When the Talmud students came to him to inquire why, so many years ago, he had told Moshe that there was no chimney sweep in Yanov, he would raise his eyebrows, shrug his shoulders and answer:

"I really don't know."

"And where do you come from?" they would ask him.

He would give some sort of reply, but his words did not come out clearly. The people thought he was deaf. And yet he had no trouble at all hearing the Reader's prayers from his remote corner of the study house. Mindel catered to him, pampering him with chicken and oatmeal, but he ate less and less as time went by. He would absently raise a spoonful of soup to his lips and then forget to put it in his mouth. The little bird which Moshe had brought with him to Yanov had long since died, but his wife had bought another bird from the gypsies. The cage was never closed, and the bird would fly out and perch on the beggar's shoulder for hours on end.

After some time had passed, the beggar was taken ill again. Moshe and his wife sent for a doctor who spared neither time nor remedies, but apparently the man had no more years left. He died during the Passover month and was buried on a Friday. The burial society set aside a plot for him among the graves of residents of long standing. Half of Yanov followed the funeral procession. When Moshe and Mindel returned home from the cemetery they found that their bird had gone. It never came back. And in Yanov the word went around that the old beggar who had died had been a *Lamed-Vavnik,* one of the Thirty-Six Righteous Men who, living out their days in obscurity, were keeping the world from destruction by the strength of their virtues.

One night, not long after the beggar's death, Moshe and his wife could not sleep. They began to speak of all sorts of things, talking on till sunrise. That morning Moshe announced in the study house that he and his wife wanted to have a new Scroll of the Law made for the community.

The scribe of Yanov labored over the Scroll for three years, and during all that time Moshe and Mindel talked of their Scroll as if it had been their only daughter. Mindel skimped and saved on household expenses, but for the Scroll she bought remnants of silk and velvet, golden thread, and she hired poor maidens to fashion these into embroidered mantelets. Moshe went all the way to Lublin to order the rollers, a crown with bells, a breastplate and a silver pointer, all to adorn the Scroll. Both the mantelets and the rollers bore the beggar's name—Abraham, the son of Chaim.

On the day the Scroll was dedicated, Moshe gave a festive meal for all the poor of Yanov. Just before dusk the guests assembled in the courtyard of the synagogue. The final sheet of the Scroll had been left incomplete, and after evening services the respected citizens of the community each bought the privilege of having one letter on the last sheet inscribed in their behalf. When all the ink had dried on the parchment and the sheet had been sewn into place, the festive procession began. A wedding canopy was spread out on its poles, and held aloft by four of the most distinguished members of the congregation. Beneath the canopy marched the rabbi, carrying the new Scroll in his arms. The little bells on the shining crown tinkled softly. The men and boys sang; the maidens held up braided candles. Waxen tapers had been lit. Moshe and his wife shone in their holiday best. Simple man that he was, Moshe had pinned his two Russian medals to his lapel. Some of the more learned congregants took this amiss and wanted to tell him in no uncertain terms to take them off, but the rabbi would not allow them to humiliate Moshe in public.

Not even the very old in the congregation could recall ever having witnessed a dedication feast like this one. Two bands played without pause. The night was mild and the moon shone brightly. The sky looked like a star-studded curtain for a Heavenly Ark. The girls and the women danced together, apart from the men. One young man strode about merrily on stilts, and a jester serenaded the host and hostess—Moshe and his wife. There was plenty of wine and ginger cake, supplied by Moshe and Mindel. The band played a real wedding march, a Shear Dance, an Angry Dance, and a Good Morning Dance; it was all just like a regular wedding feast. And then Moshe hitched up his coattails and Mindel her skirts and they danced a *Kasatzke* together, bumping fronts and backsides as they pranced about.

Moshe called out:

"The Beggar-r-r's right next to God!"

And Mindel sang out in reply:

"We are not worthy even of the dust of his feet."

Moshe and Mindel still lived on for quite a few years after this celebration. Before he died, Moshe reserved a burial place for himself next to the grave of the beggar, and he asked to have the broom, the rope and the plummet, with which he had saved the old people at the poorhouse, placed in his coffin.

And as for Mindel—each day she went to the study house and drew aside the velvet curtain of the Ark to bestow a reverent kiss upon her own beloved Scroll. Early every morning without fail, until the last day of her life, she performed this ritual. And in her last will and testament she stipulated that she be buried next to her husband and the beggar who had, after all, spoken the truth.

Translated by Gertrude Hirschler

The Man Who Came Back

You may not believe it but there are people in the world who were called back. I myself knew such a one, in our town of Turbin, a rich man. He was taken with a mortal illness, the doctors said a lump of fat had formed under his heart, God forbid it should happen to any of us. He made a journey to the hot springs, to draw off the fat, but it didn't help. His name was Alter, and his wife's name was Shifra Leah; I can see them both, as if they were standing right before my eyes.

She was lean as a stick, all skin and bones, and black as a spade; he was short and fair, with a round paunch and a small round beard. A rich man's wife, but she wore a pair of broken-down clodhoppers and a shawl thrown over her head, and was forever looking out for bargains. When she heard of a village where one could pick up cheap a measure of corn or a pot of buckwheat, she would go all the way on foot and haggle there with the peasant until he let her have it for next to nothing. I beg her pardon—but the family she came from was scum. He was a lumber merchant, a partner in the sawmill; half the town bought their lumber from him. Unlike his wife, he was fond of good living, dressing like a count, always in a shortcoat and fine leather boots. You could count each hair in his beard, it was so carefully combed and brushed.

He liked a good meal too. His old woman stinted on everything for herself—but for him no delicacy was too dear. Because he favored rich broths, with circlets of fat floating on top, she bullied the butcher, demanding fat meat, with a marrow bone thrown in, for her husband's broth with the gold coins in it, as she explained. In my time, when people got married they loved each other; who ever thought of divorce? But this Shifra Leah was so wrapped up in her Alter that people laughed in their fists. My husband this, and my husband that; heaven and earth and Alter. They had no children, and it's well known that when a woman is childless she turns all her love on her husband. The doctor said he was to blame, but who can be sure about such things?

Well, to make the story short. The man took sick and it looked bad. The biggest doctors came to see him—it didn't help; he lay in bed and sank from day to day. He still ate well, she feeding him roast pigeons and marzipans and all sorts of other delicacies, but his strength was ebbing away. One day I came to bring him a prayer book that my father—rest in peace—had sent over to him. There he lay on the sofa in a green dressing gown and white socks, a handsome figure.

He looked healthy, except that his paunch was blown up like a drum, and when he spoke he puffed and he panted. He took the prayer book from me, and gave me a cookie together with a pinch on the cheek.

A day or two later the news was that Alter was dying. The menfolk gathered; the burial society waited at the door. Well, listen to what happened. When she saw that Alter was at his final gasp, Shifra Leah ran for the doctor. But by the time she got back with the doctor in tow, there was Leizer Godl, the elder of the burial society, holding a feather to her Alter's nostrils. It was all over, they were ready to lift him off the bed, as the custom is. The instant Shifra Leah took it in, she flew into a frenzy; God help us, her screaming and wailing could be heard at the edge of town. "Beasts, murderers, thugs! Out of my house! He'll live! He'll live!" She seized a broom and began to lay about her—everybody thought she had gone out of her mind. She knelt by the corpse: "Don't leave me! Take me with you!" and ranting and raving, she shook and jostled him with lamentations louder than those you'd hear on Yom Kippur.

You know you are not allowed to shake a corpse, and they tried to restrain her, but she threw herself prone on the dead man and screeched into his ear: "Alter, wake up! Alter! Alter!" A living man couldn't have stood it—his eardrums would have burst. They were just making a move to pull her away when suddenly the corpse stirred and let out a deep sigh. She had called him back. You should know that when a person dies his soul does not go up to heaven at once. It flutters at the nostrils and longs to enter the body again, it's so used to being there. If someone screams and carries on, it may take fright and fly back in, but it seldom remains long, because it cannot stay inside a body ruined by disease. But once in a great while it does, and when that happens, you have a person who was called back.

Oh, it's forbidden. When the time comes for a man to die, he should die. Besides, one who has been called back is not like other men. He wanders about, as the saying goes, between worlds; he is here, and yet he isn't here; he would be better off in the grave. Still, the man breathes and eats. He can even live with his wife. Only one thing, he casts no shadow. They say there was a man once in Lublin who had been called back. He sat all day in the prayer house and never said a word, for twelve years; he did not even recite the Psalms. When he died at last, all that was left of him was a sack of bones. He had been rotting all those years and his flesh had turned to dust. Not much was left to bury.

Alter's case was different. He immediately began to recover, talking and wisecracking as if nothing had happened. His belly shrank, and the doctor said that the fat was gone from his heart. All Turbin was agog, people even coming from other towns to get a look at him. There was muttering that the burial society put living men into the ground; for if it was possible to call Alter back, then why not others? Perhaps others were also merely cataleptic?

Shifra Leah soon drove everyone away, she allowed no one to enter her house, not even the doctor. She kept the door locked and the curtains drawn, while she tended and watched over her Alter. A neighbor reported he was already sitting up, taking food and drink, and even looking into his account books.

Well, my dear people, it wasn't a month before he showed up at the market place, with his cane and his pampered beard and his shiny boots. Folks greeted him, gathering round and wishing him health, and he answered, "So you thought you were rid of me, eh? Not so soon! Plenty of water will yet run under the bridge before I go." People asked. "What happened after you stopped breathing?" And he said: "I ate of the Leviathan and dipped it in mustard." He was always ready with the usual wisecrack. It was said that the Rabbi summoned him and they were locked up together in the judgment chamber. But no one ever knew what talk passed between them.

Anyhow, it was Alter, only now he had a nickname: the One Who Was Called Back. He was soon back at his trading in boards and logs. The gravediggers' brethren went about with long faces; they had hoped to pick up a juicy bone at the funeral. At first people were a bit afraid of him. But what was there to be afraid of? He was the same merchant. His illness had cost quite a sum, but he had enough left over. On Saturdays he came to prayer, he was called to the reading, offered thanksgiving. He was also expected to contribute to the poorhouse and to give a feast for the townsfolk, but Alter played dumb. As for his wife, Shifra Leah, she strutted like a peacock, looking down her nose at everyone. A small matter?—she had brought a dead man back to life! Ours was quite a big town. Other men fell ill and other wives tried to call them back, but no one had a mouth like hers. If everybody could be recalled, the Angel of Death would have to put aside his sword.

Well, things took a turn. Alter had a partner in his mill, Falik Weingarten; in those days people were not called by their family names, but Falik was a real aristocrat. One day Falik came to the rabbi with a queer story: Alter, his partner, had become a swindler. He stole money from the partnership, he pulled all sorts of tricks and was trying to push him, Falik, out of the business. The rabbi couldn't believe it: when a man had gone through such an ordeal, would he suddenly become a crook? It didn't stand to reason. But Falik was not one to make up tales, and they sent for Alter. He went into a song and dance—black was white, and white was black. He dug up ancient bills and accounts all the way back from King Sobieski's time. He showed bundles of claims. To hear him tell it, his partner still owed *him* a small fortune, and what's more, he threatened to start court action.

The townspeople tried arguing with Alter: "You've done business together for so many years, what's gone wrong all of a sudden?" But Alter was a changed man—he seemed to be looking for quarrels. He started litigation, and the case dragged on and cost a fortune. Falik took it so to heart that he died. Who won, I don't remember, I only remember that the sawmill went over to creditors, and Falik's widow was left penniless. The rabbi rebuked Alter: "Is this how you thank the Lord for putting you back on your feet and raising you from the dead?" Alter's answer was no better than the barking of a dog: "It was not God who did it. It was Shifra Leah." And he said further: "There is no other world. I was good and dead, and I can tell you there is nothing—no hell and no paradise." The rabbi decided he had lost his mind—perhaps so. But wait, hear the rest.

His wife, Shifra Leah, was the worst kind of draggletail—people said that a pile of dirt sprang up wherever she stood. Suddenly Alter began to demand that she should dress up, deck herself out. "A wife's place," he said, "is not only under the quilt. I want you to go promenading with me on Lublin Street." The whole town buzzed. Shifra Leah ordered a new cotton dress made, and on Sabbath afternoon, after the *cholent* meal, there were Alter and his wife Shifra Leah on the promenade, along with the tailors' helpers and shoemakers' apprentices. It was a sight—whoever had the use of his limbs ran out to look.

Alter even trimmed his beard. He became—what's it called? an atheist. Nowadays, they're all over the place; every fool puts on a short jacket and shaves his chin. But in my time we had only one atheist—the apothecary. People began to say that when Shifra Leah called Alter back with her screams, the soul of a stranger had entered his body. Souls come flying when someone dies, souls of kinsfolk and others, and, who knows, evil souls too, ready to take possession. Reb Arieh Vishnitzer, a pupil of the old rabbi, declared that Alter was no longer Alter. True, it was not the same Alter. He talked differently, he laughed differently, he looked at you differently. His eyes were like a hawk's, and when he stared at a woman, it was enough to make a shudder pass through you. He hung out with the musicians and all sorts of riffraff. At first his wife said amen to everything, whatever Alter said or did was all right with her. I beg her pardon, but she was a cow. But then a certain female arrived in our town, from Warsaw. She came to visit her sister, who wasn't much to boast of and whose husband was a barber; on market days he shaved the peasants, and he also bled them. You can expect anything from such people: he had a cage full of birds, twittering all day long, and he also had a dog. His own wife had never shaved off her hair, and the sister from Warsaw was a divorcee—no one knew who her husband was. She came among us bedecked and bejeweled, but who ever looked at her twice? A broomstick can be dressed up too. She showed the women the long stockings she was wearing, hooked, if you'll pardon the word, to her drawers. It was not hard to guess that she had come to trap some man. And who do you think fell into her clutches? Alter. When the townsfolk heard that Alter was running around with the barber's sister-in-law, they couldn't believe it; even coopers and skinners, in those days, had some regard for decency. But Alter was a changed man. God forbid, he had lost all shame. He strolled with the divorcee in the market place, and people looked from all the windows, shaking their heads and spitting in disgust. He went with her to the tavern, for all the world like a peasant with his woman. There they sat, in the middle of the week, guzzling wine.

When Shifra Leah heard it, she knew she was in trouble. She came running to the tavern, but her husband turned on her with the vilest abuse. The newcomer, the slut, also jeered at her and taunted her. Shifra Leah tried to appeal to him: "Have you no shame before the world?" "The world can kiss what we sit on," says he. Shifra Leah cried to the other one: "He is my husband!" "Mine, also," answers she. The tavern keeper tried to put a word in, but Alter and the slut belabored him too; a woman depraved is worse than the worst man. She opened such a mouth that she shocked even the tavern keeper. People said she grabbed a pitcher and threw it at him. Turbin is not Warsaw. The town was in an uproar. The rabbi sent the sexton to summon Alter to him, but Alter refused to come. Then the community threatened him with thc three letters of excommunicaion. It didn't help, he had connections with the authorities and defied one and all.

After a couple of weeks, the divorced slut left town, and people thought things would quiet down. Before the week was out, the man who was called back from the dead came to his wife with a tale. He had an opportunity, he said, to buy a wood in Wolhynia, an unusual bargain, and he must leave at once. He collected all his money, and told Shifra Leah that he had to pawn her jewelry too. He bought a barouche and two horses. People suspected he was up to something crooked and warned his wife, but the faith she had in him, he could have been a wonder rabbi. She packed his suits and underwear; roasted chickens and prepared jams for him for the journey. Just before he set off he handed her a small box: "In here," he said, "are three promissory notes. On Thursday, eight days from today, take the notes to the rabbi. The money was left with him." He spun her a story, and she swallowed it. Then he was off.

Thursday, eight days later, she opened the box and discovered a writ of divorce. She let out a scream and fell into a faint. When she came to, she ran to the Rabbi, but he took one look at the paper and said: "There is nothing to be done. A writ of divorce can be hung on your doorknob, or it can be slipped under your door." You can imagine what went on in Turbin that day. Shifra Leah pulled at her cheeks, screaming: "Why didn't I let him croak? May he drop dead whereever he is!" He had cleaned her out—even her holiday kerchief was gone. The house was there still, but it was mortgaged to the barber. In olden times, runners would have been sent after such a shameless betrayer. The Jews once had power and authority, and there was a pillory in the synagogue court, to which a wretch would have been bound. But among our Gentile officials a Jew was of small consequence—they couldn't care less. Besides, Alter had taken care to bribe his way.

Well, Shifra Leah took sick, climbed into her bed and refused to get up. She would take nothing to eat, and kept cursing him with the deadliest curses. Then suddenly she started beating her breast and lamenting: "It's all my fault. I did not do enough to please him." She wept and she laughed —she was like one possessed by an evil spirit. The barber, who claimed now to be the legal owner of the house, wanted to throw her out of her home, but the community wouldn't let him, and she remained, in a room in the attic.

In time, after a few weeks, she recovered, and she went out with a peddler's pack, like a man, to trade among the peasants. She turned out to be a good hand at buying and selling; soon the matchmakers were approaching her with proposals of marriage. She wouldn't hear of it; all she talked about, she bent your ear if you would listen, was her Alter. "You wait," she said, "he'll come back to me. The other one didn't want him, she was after his money. She'll clean him out and leave him flat." "And you'd take such riffraff back again?" folks asked her, to which she answered: "Only let him come. I'll wash his feet and drink the water." She still had a trunk left and she collected linens and woolens, like a bride. "This will be my dowry for when he returns," she boasted. "I'll marry him again." Nowadays you call it infatuation; we called it plumb crazy.

Whenever people came from the big cities, she ran to them: "Have you run into my Alter?" But no one had seen him: it was rumored that he had become an apostate. Some said he had married a she-demon. Such things happen. The years went by, and people began to think that Alter would never be heard of again.

One Sabbath afternoon, when Shifra Leah was dozing on her bench-bed (she had never learned to read the Holy Book, as the women do), the door opened and in stepped a soldier. He took out a sheet of paper. "Are you Shifra Leah, the wife of the scoundrel Alter?" She turned white as chalk; she could not understand Russian, and an interpreter was brought in. Well, Alter was in prison, a serious crime, because he was sentenced to life. He was being kept in the Lublin jail, and he had managed to bribe the soldier, who was going home on leave, to bring a letter to Shifra Leah. Who knows where Alter got the money to bribe in prison? He must have hidden it somewhere in his cot when he was first brought in. Those who read the letter said that it would have melted a stone; he wrote to his former wife: "Shifra Leah, I have sinned against you. Save me! Save me! I am going under. Death is better than such a life." The other one, the slut, the barber's sister-in-law, had stripped him of everything and left him only his shirt. She probably informed on him too.

The town buzzed with excitement. But what could anyone do to help him?—you may be sure he was not put away for reading the Holy Book. But Shifra Leah ran to all the important people in town. "It is not his fault," she cried, "it comes from his sickness." She was not yet sobered up, the old cow. People asked her: "What do you need that lecher for?" She would not allow a speck to fall on his name. She sold everything, even her Passover dishes; she borrowed money, she got what she could from high and low. Then she took herself off to Lublin, and there she must have turned heaven and earth, for she finally got him freed from jail.

Back she came to Turbin with him, and young and old ran out to meet them. When he stepped out from the covered wagon, you couldn't recognize him: without a beard, only a thick mustache, and he had on a short caftan and high boots. It was a *goy*, not Alter. On looking closer, you saw that it was Alter after all: the same walk, the same swagger. He called each man by his name and asked about all kinds of detail. He wisecracked and said things to make the women blush. They asked him: "Where's your beard?" He answers: "I pawned it with a moneylender." They asked him: "How does a Jew take up such ways?" He replies: "Are you any better? Everybody is a thief." On the spot he gave a recital of everybody's secret sins. It was plain to see that he was in the hands of the Evil One.

Shifra Leah tried to make excuses for him and to restrain him; she fluttered over him like a mother hen. She forgot that they were divorced and wanted to take him home, but the rabbi sent word that they must not live under the same roof; it was even wrong for her, he said, to have traveled with him in the same wagon. Alter might scoff at Jewishness, but the law still remained. The women took a hand. The pair were separated for twelve days, while she took the prescribed ablutions, and then they were led under the wedding canopy. A bride must go to the ritual bath even if she is taking back her own husband.

Well, a week after the wedding he started thieving. On market days he was among the carts, picking pockets. He went off to the villages to steal horses. He was no longer plump, but lean as a hound. He clambered over roofs, forced locks, broke open stable doors. He was strong as iron and nimble as a devil. The peasants got together and posted a watch with dogs and lanterns. Shifra Leah was ashamed to show her face and kept her window shuttered; you can imagine what must have gone on between man and wife. Soon Alter became the leader of a band of roughnecks. He guzzled at the tavern with them, and they sang a Polish song in his honor; I remember the words to this day: "Our Alter is a decent sort, he hands out beer by the quart."

There is a saying: a thief will end up on the gallows.

One day, as Alter was drinking with his toughs, a squadron of Cossacks came riding up to the tavern with drawn swords. Orders had come from the governor to throw him into irons and bring him to the jail. Alter saw at once that this was the end, and he grabbed a knife; his drinking pals ran off—they left him to fight it out alone. The tavern keeper said afterwards that he fought with the strength of a demon, chopping away at the Cossacks as though they were a field of cabbages. He turned over tables and threw barrels at them; he was no longer a young man, but for a while it almost looked as though he might get the better of them all. Still, as the saying goes, one is none. The Cossacks slashed and hacked at him till there was no more blood left in his veins. Someone brought the bad news to Shifra Leah, and she came running like crazy to his side. There he lay, and she wanted to call him back again, but he said one word to her: "Enough!" Shifra Leah fell silent. The Jews ransomed his body from the officials.

I didn't see him dead. But those who did swore that he looked like an old corpse that had been dug up from the grave. Pieces were dropping from his body. The face could not be recognized, it was a shapeless pulp. It was said that when he was being cleansed for burial, an arm came off, and then a foot; I wasn't there, but why should people lie? Men who are called back rot while they are alive. He was buried in a sack outside the graveyard fence, at midnight. After his death, an epidemic struck our town, and many innocent children died. Shifra Leah, that deluded woman, put up a stone for him and went to visit his grave. What I mean to say is—it is not proper to recall the dying. If she had let him go at his appointed hour, he would have left behind a good name. And who knows how many men who were called back are out in the world today? All our misfortunes come from them.

Translated by Mirra Ginsburg

A Piece of Advice

Talk about a holy man! Our powers are not theirs; their ideas are not for us to understand! But let me tell you what happened to my own father-in-law.

At the time, I was still a young man, a mere boy, and a follower of the rabbi of Kuzmir—who was there more worthy? My father-in-law lived in Rachev, where I boarded with him. He was a wealthy man and ran his house in a grand manner. For instance, look at what happened at meal times. Only *after* I had washed my hands and said the blessing, did my mother-in-law take the rolls from the oven. So that they were still hot and fresh! She timed it to the very second. In my soup, she put hardboiled eggs. I wasn't accustomed to such luxuries. In my own home the loaves of bread were baked two weeks in advance. I used to rub garlic on a slice, and wash it down with cold well water.

But at my father-in-law's everything was fancy—brass door latches, copper pans. You had to wipe your boots on a straw mat before crossing the threshold. And the fuss that was made about brewing coffee with chicory! My mother-in-law was descended from a family of Misnagids—the enemies of the Hasids—and to Misnagids the pleasures of this world mean something.

My father-in-law was an honest Jew, a Talmudic scholar; also a dealer in timber, and a mathematician of sorts. He used to have his own hut in the forest; and took a gun and two dogs when he went there, because of robbers. He knew logarithms; and by tapping the bark of a tree with his hammer, could tell if the tree were as sound inside as out. He knew how to play a game of chess with a Gentile squire. Whenever he had a free moment, he read one of the Holy Books. He carried the "Duty of the Heart" about with him in his pocket. He smoked a long pipe with an amber mouthpiece and a silver cover. He kept his prayer shawl in a hide bag, and for his phylacteries he owned silver cases.

He had two faults. First of all, he was a fervent Misnagid. What a Misnagid—he burned like fire! He called the Hasids "the heretics" and he was not ashamed to speak evil of the saintly Baal Shem himself. The first time I heard him talk like that I shuddered. I wanted to pack up and run away. But the rabbi of Kuzmir was against divorce. You married your wife, not your father-in-law. And he told me Jethro, Moses' father-in-law, hadn't been a Hasid either. I was amazed. Jethro later became a holy man. But that's putting the cart before the horse. . . .

My father-in-law's second fault was his uncontrollable anger. He had been able to conquer all his other moral weaknesses, but not that one. If a merchant did not repay a debt on time and to the penny, he called him a swindler and refused to have any further dealings with him. If the town shoemaker made him a pair of boots, and they were a little too tight or too loose, he harangued him heartlessly.

Everything had to be just so. He had gotten it into his head that Jewish homes had to be as clean as those of the Christian squires, and he insisted that his wife let him inspect the pots and pans. If there was a spot on them, he was furious. There was a joke about him: that he had discovered a hole in a potato grater! His family loved him; the town respected him. But how much bad temper can people take? Everybody became his enemy. His business partners left him. Even my mother-in-law couldn't stand it any more.

Once I borrowed a pen from him. I forgot to return it immediately, and when he wanted to write a letter to Lublin, he began hunting. Remembering that I had it, I hastened to give it back. But he had fallen into such a rage that he struck me in the face. Well, if one's own father does a thing like that, it's his privilege. But for a father-in-law to strike a son-in-law: it's unheard of! My mother-in-law became sick from what had happened; my wife wept bitterly. I myself wasn't that upset: What was the tragedy? But I saw that my father-in-law was eating his heart out, regretting it. So I went to him. "Father-in-law," I said. "Don't take it to heart. I forgive you."

As a rule he spoke very little to me. Because if he was particular about everything, I was lax. When I took off my coat, I never remembered where I had put it. If I was given some coins, I promptly misplaced them. And though Rachev was a tiny village, when I went beyond the market place, I could no longer find my way back. The houses were all alike, and I never looked at the women within. When I got lost, I would open a cottage door and ask, "Doesn't my father-in-law live here?" Those inside would always begin to titter and laugh. Finally I took a vow never to walk anywhere except straight from my home to the study house and back again. —Only later did it occur to me that near my father-in-law's house stood a landmark: a thick tree with deep roots, which must have been two hundred years old.

Anyway, for one reason or another, my father-in-law and I were always quarreling, and he avoided me. But after the incident of the pen, he talked to me. "Baruch, what shall I do?" he said. "I'm a bad-tempered man. I know the sin of anger is as evil as that of idolatry. For years I've tried to control my temper, yet it only gets worse. I'm sinking into hell. In worldly matters too, it's very bad. My enemies want to destroy me. I'm afraid I'll end up without bread in the house."

I answered: "Father-in-law, come with me to Rabbi Chazkele of Kuzmir."

He turned pale. "Have you gone mad?" he shouted. "You know I don't believe in wonder-rabbis!"

I held my tongue. First, because I didn't want him to scold me as he always regretted it later. And, second, I didn't want him to go on slandering a holy man.

Imagine then: After the evening prayer, he came over to me and said: "Baruch, we're going to Kuzmir." I was stupefied. But why go into that. . . . He had decided to go, and we began to prepare for the journey immediately. As it was winter, we had to hire a sleigh. A deep snow had fallen and the road was far from safe; the forests were full of wolves; nor was there any lack of highwaymen. But we had to go right away. Such was my father-in-law's nature! My mother-in-law thought—heaven forbid—that he had lost his mind. He put on his fur coat, a pair of straw overshoes, and said the special prayer for a journey. I found the whole thing a great adventure. Wasn't I going to Kuzmir and taking my father-in-law with me? Who could be happier than I? Yet I trembled with fear, for who knew what would happen there!

On the journey, my father-in-law didn't utter a word. It snowed the whole way. The fields as we passed were full of swirling snowflakes. Philosophers say the shape of each flake is unique. But snow is a subject in itself. It comes from Heaven and lets us experience the peace of the other world. White is the color of mercy according to the cabala, while red signifies the law.

Nowadays snow is a trifle: it falls for a day or two at most. But in those days! Often it snowed for a month without stopping! Huge snowdrifts piled up; houses were buried; and everyone had to dig their way out. Heaven and earth merged and became one. Why does the beard of an old man turn white? Such things are all related. —At night, we heard the howling of beasts . . . or perhaps it was only the sound of the wind.

We arrived in Kuzmir on a Friday afternoon. My father-in-law went to the rabbi's study to greet him. He was permitted to go in immediately. Since it was the middle of winter, few of the rabbi's disciples had come. I waited in the study house, my skin tingling. My father-in-law was by nature such a bullheaded man. He might very well talk back to Rabbi Chazkele. It was three-quarters of an hour before he came out, his face white as chalk above his long beard, his eyes burning like coals beneath his bushy eyebrows.

"If it wasn't the eve of the Sabbath, I would go home immediately," he said.

"What happened, father-in-law?" I asked.

"Your wonder-rabbi is a fool! An ignoramus! If he weren't an old man, I would tear off his sidelocks."

The taste of gall was strong in my mouth; and I regretted the whole affair. To talk this way about Rabbi Chazkele of Kuzmir!

"Father-in-law," I asked, "what did the rabbi say to you?"

"He told me to become a flatterer," my father-in-law answered. "For eight days I must flatter everyone I meet, even the worst scoundrel. If your rabbi had an ounce of sense he would know that I hate flattery like the plague. It makes me sick even to come in contact with it. For me, a flatterer is worse than a murderer."

"Well, father-in-law," said I, "do you think the rabbi doesn't know that flattery is bad? Believe me, he knows what he's doing."

"What does he know? One sin cannot wipe out another. He knows nothing about the law."

I went away completely crushed. I had not yet been to the ritual bath, so I went there. I have forgotten to mention that my father-in-law never went to the ritual bath. I don't know why. I guess it's the way of the Misnagids. He was haughty perhaps. It was beneath his dignity to undress among other men. When I came out of the ritual bath, the Sabbath candles were already lit. Rabbi Chazkele used to bless the Sabbath candles long before dark—he himself, not his wife. His wife lit her own candles. But that's another matter. . . .

I entered the study house. The rabbi was standing in his white gabardine and his white hat. His face shone like the sun. One could see clearly he was in a higher world. When he sang out, "Give thanks unto the Lord for He is good for His mercy endureth forever," the walls shook. While praying the rabbi clapped his hands and stamped his feet.

Only a few disciples were present. But they were the elite, men of holy deeds, every one of them a personal friend of the rabbi. As they chanted, I felt their prayers reaching the heavens. Never, not even at Kuzmir, had I experienced such a beginning of the holy Sabbath. The rejoicing was so real that you could touch it. All their eyes were shining. My mind became so light that I could barely keep my feet on the ground. I happened to be praying near a window. Snow had covered everything—no road, no path, no cottages. Candles seemed to burn in the snow. Heaven and earth were one. The moon and the stars touched the roofs. Those who were not in Kuzmir that Friday evening will never know what this world can be. . . . I'm not speaking now of the world to come. . . .

I glanced at my father-in-law. He stood in a corner, his head bent. As a rule, his sternness was visible in his face, but now he looked humble, quite a different person. After the prayers we went to eat at the rabbi's table.

The rabbi had put on a white robe of silk, with silver fasteners, and embroidered with flowers. As his custom was before the Sabbath meal, he now sat alone in his library, reciting chapters of the Mishnah and of the Zohar. The older disciples sat down on benches; the younger men, I among them, stood about.

When the rabbi came out of his study, he intoned the verses, "Peace be with you," and "A woman of worth, who can find?" Then he blessed the wine and said a prayer over the white bread of the Sabbath. He ate a morsel no bigger than an olive. Immediately thereafter, he began the Sabbath table chants. But this wasn't mere chanting! His body swayed; he cooed like a dove; it sounded like the singing of angels. His communion with God was so complete that his soul almost left his body. Everybody could see that the holy man was not here but high up in heaven.

Who knows what heights he reached? How can one describe it? As the Talmud says, "He who has not seen joy like this has never seen joy at all." He was at the same time at the court in Kuzmir, and high above in God's temples, in the Nest of the Bird, at the Throne of Glory. Such rapture is impossible to imagine. I forgot about my father-in-law and even about myself. I was no longer Baruch from Rachev—but bodiless, sheer nothing. It was one o'clock in the morning before we left the rabbi's table. Such a Sabbath service never happened before and never will again—maybe, when the Messiah comes.

But I am forgetting the main thing. The rabbi commented on the law. And what he said was connected with what he had told my father-in-law at their meeting. "What should a Jew do if he is not a pious man?" the Rabbi asked. And answered: "Let him play the pious man. The Almighty does not require good intentions. The deed is what counts. It is what you do that matters. Are you angry perhaps? Go ahead and be angry, but speak gentle words and be friendly at the same time. Are you afraid of being a dissembler? So what if you pretend to be something you aren't? For whose sake are you lying? For your Father in Heaven. His Holy Name, blessed be He, knows the intention and the intention behind the intention, and it is this that is the main thing."

How can one convey the rabbi's lesson? Pearls fell from his mouth and each word burned like fire and penetrated the heart. It wasn't so much the words themselves, but his gestures and his tone. The evil spirit, the rabbi said, cannot be conquered by sheer will. It is known that the evil one has no body, and works mainly through the power of speech. Do not lend him a mouth—that is the way to conquer him. Take, for example, Balaam, the son of Beor. He wanted to curse the children of Israel but forced himself to bless them instead, and because of this, his name is mentioned in the Bible. When one doesn't lend the evil one a tongue, he must remain mute.

Why should I ramble on? My father-in-law attended all three Sabbath meals. And when, on the Sabbath night, he went to the rabbi to take leave of him, he stayed in his study for a whole hour.

On the way home, I said, "Well, father-in-law?" And he answered: "Your rabbi is a great man."

The road back to Rachev was full of dangers. Though it was still midwinter, the ice on the Vistula had cracked—ice-blocks were floating downstream the way they do at Passover time. In the midst of all the cold, thunder and lightning struck. No doubt about it, only Satan could be responsible for this! We were forced to put up at an inn until Tuesday—and there were many Misnagids staying there. No one could travel further. A real blizzard was raging outside. The howling in the chimney made you shiver.

Misnagids are always the same. These were no exception. They began to heap ridicule upon Hasids—but my father-in-law maintained silence. They tried to provoke him but he refused to join in. They took him to task: "What about this one? What about that one?" He put them off good-naturedly with many tricks. "What change has come over you?" they asked. If they had known that he was coming from Rabbi Chazkele, they would have devoured him.

What more can I tell you? My father-in-law did what the Rabbi had prescribed. He stopped snapping at people. His eyes glowed with anger but his speech was soft. And if at times he lifted his pipe about to strike someone, he always stopped himself and spoke with humility. It wasn't long before the people of Rachev realized that my father-in-law was a changed man. He made peace with his enemies. He would stop any little brat in the street and give him a pinch on the cheek. And if the water carrier splashed water entering our house, though I knew this just about drove my father-in-law crazy, he never showed it. "How are you, Reb Yontle?" he would say. "Are you cold, eh?" One could feel that he did this only with great effort. That's what made it noble.

In time, his anger disappeared completely. He began to visit Rabbi Chazkele three times a year. He became a kindly man, so good-natured it was unbelievable. But that is what a habit is like—if you break it, it becomes the opposite. One can turn the worst sin into a good deed. The main thing is to act, not to ponder. He even began to visit the ritual bath. And when he grew old, he acquired disciples of his own. This was after the death of Rabbi Chazkele. My father-in-law always used to say, "If you can't be a good Jew, act the good Jew, because if you act something, you *are* it. Otherwise why does any man try to act at all? Take, for example, the drunk in the tavern. Why doesn't he try to act differently?"

The rabbi once said: "Why is 'Thou Shalt Not Covet' the very last of the Ten Commandments? Because one must first avoid doing the wrong things. Then, later on, one will not desire to do them. If one stopped and waited until all the passions ceased, one could never attain holiness."

And so it is with all things. If you are not happy, act the happy man. Happiness will come later. So also with faith. If you are in despair, act as though you believed. Faith will come afterwards.

Translated by Martha Glicklich
and Joel Blocker

In the Poorhouse

I

There was a warm, homelike feeling about the poorhouse today. The rich man of the town, Reb Leizer Lemkes, married off his youngest daughter, Altele. And he gave a feast for the poor. In addition to gorging themselves on carp, *kreplach* with soup, *chalah*, beef and carrot stew, and washing it all down with wine, each of the paupers was given something to take home: a slice of honey cake, a chicken drumstick, an apple, a piece of pastry. Everyone had eaten his fill. Most of them had overeaten. The poorhouse overseer had also had his share and did not stint today: he piled the stove full of firewood. Such heat came from its iron door that Hodele the beggar asked someone to open the chimney, she was in such a sweat.

After the feast everybody fell asleep. Night descended quickly. None of the men had prayed that evening. But after some hours of sleep, the little family began to wake. First to open his eyes was Leibush Scratch. He had hidden a roast chicken in the straw. And he began to put it away now, for fear that someone might steal it during the long night, or else the mice might get at it.

The second to wake up was Jonah the Thief. He had slipped under his pillow a head of a carp wrapped in cabbage leaves—a present from Serele the servant girl. Bashe the Whore, who had hidden three macaroons in her stocking, could not sleep either. The sounds of munching, chewing, gnawing mingled with the snuffling and snoring of the sleepers. Outside, fresh snow had fallen, and the moon was bright. After a while, Leibush Scratch asked:

"Jonah, my friend, are you eating or sleeping on it?"

"Chewing is no sin," Jonah the Thief retorted smartly.

"Leave him alone, Reb Leibush," put in Bashe the Whore, "or he may swallow a bone."

"What are you crunching there?" asked Leibush. "Last Passover's matzos?"

"A bit of a macaroon."

"I thought you had something. Who gave it to you, eh?"

"The little Tsipele."

"Give me a piece. . . ."

Bashe did not answer.

Jonah the Thief laughed: "Her kind doesn't give anything for nothing."

"I can give her my bellyache."

"If you have an ache, you can keep it to yourself," replied Bashe.

"I have plenty to spare for you too."

"Don't curse, Reb Leibush, I am cursed enough," said Bashe. At any other time she would not trouble to talk to Leibush, but the food and the wine and the glowing stove softened all hearts. People forgot their quarrels for a while. Besides, the night was long, and they could not go back to sleep.

For a while it was quiet again. Leibush could be heard cracking the chicken bones and sucking the marrow. Then he asked:

"I wonder how late it is?"

"I sent my watch for repair," joked Jonah the Thief.

"Once upon a time I had no need of watches. In the daytime I could tell the hour by the sun. At night I looked at the stars, or sniffed the wind. But you can't tell anything in this stench. Why are no roosters crowing?"

"All the roosters were slaughtered for the wedding," said Bashe.

"Tell us a story, Reb Leibush," asked Jonah the Thief.

"What story? I've told you everything. Old Getsl makes up his stories, but I don't like to make them up. What's the good of that? I can tell you that I was Count Pototsky once upon a time, or that Radziwill used to heat the bath house for me. What will come of that? Did I ever tell you about the mannikin?"

"In the glass of whiskey? With the magician?"

"Yes."

"You told us that one."

"And about the hail?"

"The hail too."

"And the ox?"

"The way the ox attacked you on the way to night prayers?"

"Yes."

"You did, you told us that one too."

"Well, what can I tell you, then? You are a thief, you have many stories to tell. I spent my life over the grindstone."

"Hey, you, Bashe, why don't you ever tell us anything?" asked Jonah.

Bashe was silent. They no longer expected her to answer. Suddenly her voice was heard:

"What can I tell you?"

"Tell us how you became a whore, and all the rest of it."

"The moment I open my mouth, the women begin to curse."

"The women are asleep."

"They'll wake soon enough. They don't let me live. God has forgiven long ago, but they won't forgive. What harm have I done them? I am not from these parts. I have never sinned with their husbands. I lie here and never hurt a fly, but they eat me up alive with their eyes. They spit into my face. Whenever anyone brings a plate of soup or a bowl of *kashe*, they begin to hiss like snakes: 'Not for her! Not for her!' If it were up to them, I would have died of hunger long ago. But kind people have pity. If I had my legs, I'd not be lying here. I'd run from here to where black pepper grows."

"But you have none."

"And that's my bitter misfortune. I long for death, but it doesn't come. Healthy people go, but I lie here and rot alive. It's lucky they put me here. The women used to pinch me, they used to tear out lumps of my flesh. They threw garbage at me. They spilled their night slops over me. . . ."

"We know, we know it all."

"You don't know one thousandth of it. When a man hits someone, everybody sees it and there's a hullaballoo. But women can dig your heart out on the sly. Now they cannot reach me with their hands, so they stick needles into me with their eyes. They can't forgive me that I lie here among the men. When I lie dead, with my feet toward the door and a straw under my head, they will still envy me."

"I thought you were going to tell us a story."

"What have I to tell? I've had troubles from my childhood on. My mother, may she intercede for me, had three daughters before me. My father wanted a boy. He made a journey to a rabbi, and the rabbi promised him a boy. When the midwife told him it was a girl, he would not believe her. He demanded to be shown. . . . My father was a Hasid, and it was a custom in the study house that a man whose wife gave birth to one daughter after another was given a whipping. The Hasidim stretched my father out on the table, and whipped him with their sashes. He never wanted to look at me. He would not even call me by my name. He never hit me either. Just as if I were a step-child. When I called him 'father,' he pretended he did not hear me. Was it my fault? My mother used to say: 'You were born in a black hour.' When I was nine, I left home."

"Why did you leave home?"

"Because I slaughtered three ducks."

"What? You slaughtered ducks?"

"Yes, I was growing up a wild thing. Whatever I saw, I imitated. One day my mother sent me to the *shochet*, to have him slaughter a hen. I saw him standing there with the knife slaughtering the fowl, and I liked it. We had three ducks locked in the pantry. I took a pocket knife, spit on a stone, sharpened it, and cut the throats of the three ducks. Suddenly the door opened, and my father came in. He turned white as chalk. He ran to my mother, screaming: 'Either she goes, or I do . . .' On the following day they packed a few things into a bundle and sent me into service in Lublin."

"But how did you become a whore?"

"How did you become a horse thief? Little by little. A young fellow promises to lead you under the bridal canopy. Then he tells you to go and whistle."

"Who was the first one?"

"A teacher's helper."

"A teacher's helper, eh? And then?"

"He went away, and that was the last of him. Try and find a teacher's helper in God's world. After him came a tailor's assistant, and after the tailor, a hat-maker. When a girl loses her virtue, she is anybody's game. Whoever wants to, has the use of her. A bridal canopy is only a few lengths of velvet and four posts. But without it, a girl is less than the dirt under your nail."

"We know that. When did you enter a brothel?"

"When I got a belly full."

"And what happened there?"

"What could happen there? Nothing."

"And the child, what became of it?"

"It was left on the church steps."

"One child?"

"Three."

"And then what?"

"Nothing."

"This is no story."

"The story comes later."

"What happened?"

"I'm ashamed to tell it before Reb Leibush."

"What? But he's sleeping."

"He fell asleep?"

"Don't you hear him snoring?"

"Yes. But he was talking just now!"

"At his age you can talk one minute, doze off the next, and a minute later you make bye-bye, and it's all over. And with me you don't have to feel ashamed."

"No."

"Let's hear it, then."

"I'm afraid the women are listening."

"They're sleeping like the dead. Talk quietly. I am not deaf."

"There are times when you want to talk. I was already in Warsaw at that time. I was with a madam. She had three of us, and I was the prettiest. Don't look at me today. I am a broken vessel. I have no legs, my hair is gone, my teeth are gone. I am an old scarecrow. But in my young days I was a beauty. The queen! That's what they called me. People could not look into my face—it dazzled like the sun. Whenever a guest had me, he never wanted anyone else. The other two stood at the gate all night, but I sat on my bed and they came to me as if I were a doctor. The madam had a tongue like a whip, but when she spoke to me, it was as through a silken cloth. I had a fiancé—that's what we called them—Yankel, and he was crazy about me. He bought me whatever I wanted. If the madam said an unkind word to me, right away he'd pull the knife out of his boot. He was a wild one, too. A guest is a guest, after all. But suddenly he'd get jealous. He'd grab the man by the collar and throw him down the whole flight of stairs, if he just dared to kiss me. The madam would yell murder, but he'd yell back: 'Shut up, or I'll knock out all your teeth.' He wanted to marry me, too, but his years were short. He caught the smallpox and was covered with blisters all over. They took him in an ambulance to the hospital, and there they poisoned everybody."

"Poisoned? Why?"

"Just so."

"And then what?"

"He died and was buried. After that my luck changed. I was taken over by another fellow, but that one had only money on his mind. Sender was his name, Senderl the Bum. He did not care for me, and I did not care for him. When the madam saw that things were going badly with me, she began to lord it over me. I could not run away because I had a yellow passport. And where can our kind escape? Only to the grave. The madam began to abuse me, and the other two sluts made my life miserable. A woman must have someone to protect her, or else she's nine feet deep in trouble.

"Once in two weeks we had our day off. When Yankel was alive, he used to take me everywhere. We even drove out in a *droshky*. He bought me chocolates, marmalade, halvah and licorice from a Turk—whatever my heart desired. There was a carousel in Voiny Place, and we used to go round and round in it. But when Yankel was gone, I was all alone. The madam lived on Nizka Street, and I went out walking along the Dzhika. Were you ever in Warsaw? I had nothing to do. So I leaned on a lamp-post, cracking sunflower seeds. I was not out to catch anyone. I put on a cotton dress and a shawl over my shoulders, like an honest girl.

"I stand there, and think about my life. Suddenly a tall young man comes over to me, in a wide-brimmed hat, with a shock of long hair and a cape down to the sidewalk. I was so startled, I cried out. He looked strange, pale and disheveled like a free-thinker. In those years workers were organizing unions and throwing bombs at the Tsar. I thought he was one of that company. I wanted to get away, but he put out a long hand and grabbed me. 'Fraulein,' says he, 'do not run away. I do not eat people.' 'What does the gentleman want?'

I ask. And he says: 'Do you want to earn some money?' 'Who doesn't want money?' I say, 'But I have no time. I must be back at the old woman's in an hour.' 'It won't take an hour,' says he. He starts talking so fast that I cannot understand anything at first. He is in love, he tells me, with a girl, and she is making him sweat. So he wants me to come with him and he'll introduce me as his fiancée. 'What will come of it?' I ask, '—besides, I must get back very soon.' And he says: 'I want to test her.' 'How do you know who I am?' I ask. So he tells me he lives across the street and he sees me at the gate. It seems he followed me.

"I was afraid because I could not stay out long, and Sender was free with his fists. Anything not to his liking, and he could beat you to death. But before I could say a word, I was sitting in a *droshky*. 'Take off your shawl,' says he. On Nalewki Street there was a milliner. He tells the droshky to wait and picks out a hat for me, with a wide brim, for three roubles. I put it on, and I don't know my own face in the mirror. He takes my shawl and hides it under his cloak. We drive out on Mead Street, and there he buys me a handbag. All the customers haggle. They bargain the shopkeeper down to half the asking price. But he doesn't bargain, he pays whatever they ask. The salesgirls laugh at him and pinch one another. My mother used to say: 'Send a fool to market, and the shopkeepers rejoice.' To make it short and sweet, I was now a lady from Marshalkovski Street.

"From Mead Street we drove back to Franciscan Boulevard. The driver was already beginning to grumble that it was more than a single fare zone. So the man takes a half a rouble from his pocket and hands it to him. He is throwing money around like a lord.

"Then we come to a leather goods store, and there's a girl inside. There are no customers. He lets me walk ahead and then follows me in. Respect for the ladies, we called it in Warsaw. She was an ordinary girl. I could not tell what he saw in her. Her eyes were black and sharp. You could tell she was a shrew. She took one look at him and turned white as chalk. He takes me under the arm and leads me to the counter. 'Leah, my dear,' he says, 'this is my fiancée.' I thought the jade would catch apoplexy on the spot. If she could, she would have swallowed me up alive. 'Why did you bring your fiancée here?' she asked, 'Do you want me to congratulate her?' 'No,' he answers, 'this wasn't the reason. I want a pair of shoes made for her, and I know your father sells the best leather. Give her first-class goods. The price is no object.' If the girl did not catch a stroke, she was stronger than iron. 'You cannot buy leather without a shoemaker,' she says. 'You have to know the size and the trimmings.' 'You can take her size,' says he, and tells me to sit down on the stool. He lifts up my dress, tears off a strip of paper and measures my foot. And he says: 'Leah my dear, did you ever see such a foot? It's the smallest foot in Warsaw.' I really had small feet. He tickles me with his long fingers, and I can hardly keep a straight face. The girl says: 'Don't think you are fooling me. You could have gotten your leather somewhere else. You came here to tease me. So I can tell you: whoever begrudges you, let him have nothing himself. And she isn't your fiancée either. You picked someone up in the street. I know your tricks. I don't need your trade. Get out of here and don't come back. If you show up again, alone or with her, I'll call the policeman!' My gentleman turns white and says nothing. He drops my foot, and I sit there with one shoe and one stocking. And then he cries out: 'Yes, you are right. She is a girl from the street, but I swear to God I'll marry her this very day! Tonight she'll be my wife, and I'll forget all about you. I'll tear you from my heart. I'll love her with my whole soul. Even if she is an unfortunate one, she has more decency than you. . . .' Those were his words. He started abusing her in the vilest language. He caught me by the hand and screamed:

" 'Come to the rabbi, my bride! Tonight we shall be man and wife.'

"I was so mixed up that I left one shoe in the store."

II

Leibush Scratch woke up.

"You're talking? Talk. What happened after that?"

"Have you heard it, then?" Jonah the Thief asked. "But you were sleeping!"

"I dozed off, but I heard. At my age sleep isn't what it used to be. I dream I am at a fair, and I know I am lying here at the poorhouse. I am here, and I am there. I am Leibush, and I am the rabbi. Why did you leave your shoe, eh?"

"I was afraid a crowd would gather."

"How could you walk around in one shoe?"

"Just as I stood there, the shoe flew after me from the store. I ran to catch it, and a cart almost knocked me over. My fine gentleman dropped down on his knees in the middle of the gutter and put the shoe on my foot. Just like a play in the theatre. The whole street laughed. The *droshky* was gone, and he pulled me and yelled: 'Where do you find a rabbi around here?' People pointed out a house across the street. And then, my friends, I saw that I had no luck. We were already in front of the steps, when I was suddenly afraid. I said to him: 'You love the other girl, not me.' 'I'll love you, I'll love you,' he answers. 'I am a trained pharmacist. I can live in Petersburg, in Moscow, anywhere in Russia. We'll leave this city, and I'll pluck her out of my heart. I'll love and cherish you, and you will be the mother of my children.' I remember every word as if it happened yesterday. I did not know what a pharmacist was. Later someone explained to me it meant a druggist. An educated man. But I say: 'Do you know what I do?' 'I know,' he cries, 'but I don't want to know. I'll forgive you everything . . .' 'But you don't even know me,' I say, but he screams: 'I do not need to know you. You are more pure than she is . . .' I look at him: he is foaming at the mouth. His eyes are like a madman's. I suddenly felt sick. I broke away and began to run. I ran out of the gates, and heard him running after me and calling: 'Where are you running? Where are you running? Come back! . . .' I ran as if he were a murderer. I came to the butcher stalls in the market, and there I got away from him. The place was so crowded that you could not drop a needle. It was only after I cooled off that I realized that I was done for. Where was I running, woe is me? Back to the mire.

"When I came home and they saw me with the stylish hat and handbag, there was an uproar. The old woman asks: 'Where is the shawl?' And I don't have the shawl. He hid it under his cape. Well, there was no end of talk and laughter. They wouldn't believe me, either. When Sender came and they told him everything, he took away the hat and the handbag. He gave me a punch too, into the bargain. He had a fiancée somewhere, and he took everything to her. And, my dear people, I'll tell you something else: the old woman deducted from my wages for the shawl, or may I never have a holy burial."

For a long while everyone was silent. Then Leibush Scratch asked:

"You are sorry now, eh?"

"Why not? I wouldn't be rotting here today."

"If he lived across the street, why didn't you seek him out?" asked Jonah the Thief.

"They would not give me any days off after that. I thought he would come, but he never did."

"Perhaps he made up with the girl from the leather store?"

"Perhaps."

"There is a saying: forge the iron while it's hot," Leibush Scratch said reflectively.

"That's true."

"And yet, if it is not written for you, it isn't. Was it you, then, who was running? Your feet carried you. Or take me. Did I have to end up lying here on a bundle of straw? Not more than you have to dance on the roof. I was not rich, but I was a man of some property. I owned a house, a small mill. I had a wife . . . But if they want it up in heaven that a man should fall, they find a way. First my wife sickened and died. Then the house went up in smoke. Nobody knew how it started. A few splinters were smoldering under the tripod. Then suddenly there was a burst of fire as though hell itself had opened. There wasn't even any wind. My house stood right next to Chaim the Cooper's, but never a spark touched his place, while I was ruined. Can anyone understand that?"

"No."

"Someone saw a little flame sit on the bed. It rolled over and made somersaults. It was all from the evil ones."

"What did the evil ones have against you?"

"I was destined to take up a beggar's sack. . . ."

Jonah the Thief began to crack his knuckles, first one hand, then the other.

"Isn't it the truth, though? That night when I went to the village of Bysht I knew well enough that I should not go. The peasants had heard of me. I was warned that they were sleeping in the stables. Wojciech the village elder had posted a watch with a rattle. I needed the whole business like a hole in the head. Just a few days before that I pulled in a big haul. Zeldele, may she rest in peace, begged me: 'Jonah, don't try to grab the whole world. I'd rather eat dry bread than see you making this kind of a living.' And what did we need? There were only the two of us. Zelig the horse merchant wanted to hire me as a driver. I could have become a horse dealer myself. Sometimes you earn more, sometimes less, but it's honest money. I was already going to bed that night. I closed the shutters and pulled off my boots. Suddenly I put them on again and started out for Bysht. I walked with a heavy heart. I kept stopping and wanting to turn back. But I never walked back—they brought me home in a wheelbarrow."

"What did they do it with? Sticks?" asked Leibush.

"Whatever they could lay their hands on. A whole village against one man. . . ."

"I'll tell you the truth—it's a wonder you came out alive. This was before your day. There was a certain Itchele Nonie—that's what they called him because he had a long nose—and he went to Boyares to steal a horse. The peasants ambushed him and burned him alive. All that was left of him was a heap of ashes. The gravediggers' brotherhood had nothing to bury . . ."

"I know. I've heard of it. He had better luck than I."

"When did your wife die? I don't remember any more."

"Six months later."

"From all that trouble, eh?"

"No, from pleasure."

"Well, everything is destined. Everything is written for us above, to the last breath. As my grandmother used to say: Nobody is mightier than the Almighty."

"Who writes it all? God?"

"Not you."

"Where does he get so much paper?"

"Don't let your brains dry up in worrying about that."

"Man has his share of responsibility too."

"No, he hasn't. . . ."

It became quiet at the poorhouse. Hodele the beggar moaned in her sleep, muttered unintelligible words. A cricket chirped once. Leibush Scratch resumed his snoring, whistling through his nose. Jonah the Thief asked:

"Do you still have a piece of macaroon? I have a bitter taste in my mouth. . . ."

Bashe did not answer.

Translated by Mirra Ginsburg

The Destruction of Kreshev

I

REB BUNIM COMES TO KRESHEV

I am the Primeval Snake, the Evil One, Satan. The cabala refers to me as Samael and the Jews sometimes call me merely, "that one."

It is well-known that I love to arrange strange marriages, delighting in such mismatings as an old man with a young girl, an unattractive widow with a youth in his prime, a cripple with a great beauty, a cantor with a deaf woman, a mute with a braggart. Let me tell you about one such "interesting" union I contrived in Kreshev, which is a town on the river San, that enabled me to be properly abusive and gave me the opportunity to perform one of those little stunts that forces the forsaking of both this world and the next between the saying of a "yes" and a "no."

Kreshev is about as large as one of the smallest letters in the smallest prayer books. On two sides of the town there is a thick pine forest and on the third the river San. The peasants in the neighboring villages are poorer and more isolated than any others in the Lublin district and the fields are the most barren. During a good part of the year the roads leading to the larger towns are merely broad trenches of water; one travels by wagon at one's peril. Bears and wolves lurk at the edge of the settlement in winter and often attack a stray cow or calf, occasionally even a human being. And, finally, so that the peasants shall never be rid of their wretchedness, I have instilled in them a burning faith. In that part of the country there is a church in every other village, a shrine at every tenth house. The Virgin stands with rusty halo, holding in her arms Jesus, the infant son of the Jewish carpenter Yossel. To her the aged come—and in the depth of winter kneel down, thus acquiring rheumatism. When May comes we have daily processions of the half-starved chanting with hoarse voices for rain. The incense gives off an acrid odor, and a consumptive drummer beats with all his might to frighten me away. Nevertheless, the rains don't come. Or if they do, they are never in time. But that doesn't prevent the people from believing. And so it has continued from time immemorial.

The Jews of Kreshev are both somewhat better informed and more prosperous than the peasants. Their wives are shopkeepers and are skilled in giving false weight and measure. The village peddlers know how to get the peasant women to purchase all sorts of trinkets and thus earn for themselves corn, potatoes, flax, chickens, ducks, geese—and sometimes a little extra. What won't a woman give for a string of beads, a decorated feather duster, a flowered calico, or just a kind word from a stranger? So it is not entirely surprising that here and there among the flaxen-haired children one comes across a curly-haired, black-eyed imp with a hooked nose. The peasants are extremely sound sleepers but the devil does not permit their young women to rest but leads them down backpaths to barns where the peddlers wait in the hay. Dogs bay at the moon, roosters crow, frogs croak, the stars in heaven look down and wink, and God himself dozes among the clouds. The Almighty is old; it is no easy task to live forever.

But let us return to the Jews of Kreshev.

All year round, the market place is one deep marsh, for the very good reason that the women empty their slops there. The houses don't stand straight; they are half-sunk into the earth and have patched roofs; their windows are stuffed with rags or covered with ox bladders. The homes of the poor have no floors; some even lack chimneys. In such houses the smoke from the stove escapes through a hole in the roof. The women marry when they are fourteen or fifteen and age quickly from too much childbearing. In Kreshev the cobblers at their low benches have only worn-out, scuffed shoes on which to practice their trade. The tailors have no alternative but to turn the ragged furs brought to them to their third side. The brushmakers comb hog bristles with wooden combs and hoarsely sing fragments of ritual chants and wedding tunes. After market day there is nothing for the storekeepers to do and so they hang around the study house, scratching themselves and leafing through the Talmud or else telling each other amazing stories of monsters and ghosts and werewolves. Obviously in such a town there isn't much for me to do. One is just very hard put to come across a real sin thereabouts. The inhabitants lack both the strength and the inclination. Now and again a seamstress gossips about the rabbi's wife or the water bearer's girl grows large with child, but those are not the sort of things that amuse me. That is why I rarely visit Kreshev.

But at the time I am speaking about there were a few rich men in the town and in a prosperous home anything can happen. So whenever I turned my eyes in that direction, I made sure to see how things were going in the household of Reb Bunim Shor, the community's richest man. It would take too long to explain in detail how Reb Bunim happened to settle in Kreshev. He had originally lived in Zholkve which is a town near Lemberg. He had left there for business reasons. His interest was lumber and for a very small sum he had purchased a nice tract of woods from the Kreshev squire. In addition, his wife, Shifrah Tammar (a woman of distinguished family, granddaughter of the famous scholar Reb Samuel Edels) suffered from a chronic cough which made her spit blood, and a Lemberg doctor had recommended that she live in a wooded area. At any rate, Reb Bunim had moved to Kreshev with all his possessions, bringing along with him also a grown son and Lise, his ten-year-old daughter. He had built a house set apart from all the other dwellings at the end of the synagogue street; and several wagonloads of furniture, crockery, clothing, books and a host of other things had been crammed into the building. He had also brought with him a couple of servants, an old woman and a young man called Mendel, who acted as Reb Bunim's coachman. The arrival of the new inhabitant restored life to the town. Now there was work for the young men in Reb Bunim's forests and Kreshev's coachmen had logs to haul. Reb Bunim repaired the town's bath and he constructed a new roof for the almshouse.

Reb Bunim was a tall, powerful, large-boned man. He had the voice of a cantor and a pitch-black beard that ended in two points. He wasn't much of a scholar and could scarcely get through a chapter of the Midrash, but he always contributed generously to charity. He could sit down to a meal and finish at one sitting a loaf of bread and a six-egg omelet, washing it all down with a quart of milk. Fridays at the bath, he would climb to the highest perch and would have the attendant beat him with a bundle of twigs until it was time to light the candles. When he went into the forest he was accompanied by two fierce hounds, and he carried a gun. It was said that he could tell at a glance whether a tree was healthy or rotten. When necessary, he could work eighteen hours on end and walk for miles on foot. His wife, Shifrah Tammar, had once been very handsome, but between running to doctors and worrying about herself, she'd managed to become prematurely old. She was tall and thin, almost flat-chested, and she had a long, pale face and a beak of a nose. Her thin lips stayed forever closed and her gray eyes looked belligerently out at the world. Her periods were painful and when they came she would take to her bed as though she were mortally ill. In fact she was a constant sufferer—one moment it would be a headache, the next an abscessed tooth or pressure on her abdomen. She was not a fit mate for Reb Bunim but he was not the sort who complained. Very likely he was convinced that that was the way it was with all women since he had married when he was fifteen years old.

There isn't very much to say about his son. He was like his father—a poor scholar, a voracious eater, a powerful swimmer, an aggressive businessman. He had married a girl from Brody before his father had even moved to Kreshev and had immediately immersed himself in business. He very seldom came to Kreshev. Like his father he had no lack of money. Both of the men were born financiers. They seemed to draw money to them. The way it looked, there didn't appear to be any reason why Reb Bunim and his family would not live out their days in peace as so often happens with ordinary people who because of their simplicity are spared bad luck and go through life without any real problems.

II
THE DAUGHTER

But Reb Bunim also had a daughter, and women, as it is well known, bring misfortune.

Lise was both beautiful and well brought-up. At twelve she was already as tall as her father. She had blond, almost yellow, hair and her skin was as white and smooth as satin. At times her eyes appeared to be blue and at other times green. Her behavior was a mixture, half Polish lady, half pious Jewish maiden. When she was six her father had engaged a governess to instruct her in religion and grammar. Later Reb Bunim had sent her to a regular teacher and from the very beginning she had shown a great interest in books. On her own she had studied the Scriptures in Yiddish, and dipped into her mother's Yiddish commentary on the Pentateuch. She had also been through "The Inheritance of the Deer," "The Rod of Punishment," "The Good Heart," "The Straight Measure," and other similar books that she had found in the house. After that she had managed all by herself to pick up a smattering of Hebrew. Her father had told her repeatedly that it was not proper for a girl to study Torah and her mother cautioned her that she would be left an old maid since no one wanted a learned wife, but these warnings made little impression on the girl. She continued to study, read "The Duty of the Hearts," and Josephus, familiarized herself with the tales of the Talmud, and in addition learned all sorts of proverbs of the Tanaites and Amorites. She put no limit to her thirst for knowledge. Every time a book peddler wandered into Kreshev she would invite him to the house and buy whatever he had in his sack. After the Sabbath meal her contemporaries, the daughters of the best families of Kreshev, would drop in for a visit. The girls would chatter, play odds and evens, set each other riddles to answer and act as giddily as young girls generally do. Lise was always very polite to her friends, would serve them Sabbath fruits, nuts, cookies, cakes, but she never had much to say—her mind was concerned with weightier matters than dresses and shoes. Yet her manner was always friendly, without the slightest trace of haughtiness in it. On holidays Lise went to the women's synagogue although it was not customary for girls of her age to attend services. On more than one occasion, Reb Bunim, who was devoted to her, would say sorrowfully: "It's a shame that she's not a boy. What a man she would have made."

Shifrah Tammar's feelings were otherwise.

"You're just ruining the girl," she would insist. "If this continues she won't even know how to bake a potato."

Since there was no competent teacher of secular subjects in Kreshev (Yakel, the community's only teacher, could just about write a single line of legible Yiddish), Reb Bunim sent his daughter to study with Kalman the Leech. Kalman was highly esteemed in Kreshev. He knew how to burn out elf-locks, apply leeches, and do operations with just an ordinary breadknife. He owned a caseful of books and manufactured his own pills from the herbs in the field. He was a short, squat man with an enormous belly and as he walked his great weight seemed to make him totter. He looked like one of the local gentry in his plush hat, velvet caftan, knee-length trousers and shoes with buckles. It was the custom in Kreshev to have the procession, taking the bride to the ritual bath, stop for a moment in front of Kalman's porch to serenade him gaily.

"Such a man," it was said in town, "must be kept in a good humor. All one can hope is that one never needs him."

But Reb Bunim did need Kalman. The Leech was in perpetual attendance upon Shifrah Tammar, and not only did he treat the mother's ailments, but he permitted the daughter to borrow books from his library. Lise read through his whole collection: tomes about medicine, travel books describing distant lands and savage peoples, romantic stories of the nobility, how they hunted and made love, the brilliant balls they gave. Nor was this all. In Kalman's library were also marvelous yarns about sorcerers and strange animals, about knights, kings and princes. Yes, every line of all this Lise read.

Well, now it is time for me to speak about Mendel, Mendel the man-servant—Mendel the Coachman. No one in Kreshev knew quite where this Mendel had come from. One story was that he'd been a love child who'd been abandoned in the streets. Others said he was the child of a convert. Whatever his origins, he was certainly an ignoramus and was famous not only in Kreshev but for miles around. He literally didn't know his Alef Beth, nor had he ever been seen to pray, although he did own a set of phylacteries. On Friday night all the other men would be at the House of Prayer but Mendel would be loitering in the market place. He would help the servant girls draw water from the well and would hang around the horses in the stables. Mendel shaved, had discarded his fringed garment, offered no benedictions; he had completely emancipated himself from Jewish custom. On his first appearance in Kreshev, several people had interested themselves in him. He'd been offered free instruction. Several pious ladies had warned him that he'd end up reclining on a bed of nails in Gehenna. But the young man had ignored everyone. He just puckered up his lips and whistled impudently. If some woman assailed him too vigorously, he would snarl back arrogantly: "O you cossack of God, you. Anyway you won't be in my Gehenna."

And he would take the whip that he always carried with him and use it to hike up the woman's skirt. There would be a great deal of commotion and laughter and the pious lady would vow never again to tangle with Mendel the Coachman.

Though he was a heretic that didn't prevent him from being handsome. No, he was very good-looking, tall and lithe, with straight legs and narrow hips and dense black hair which was a little bit curly and a little kinky and in which there were always a few stalks of hay and straw. He had heavy eyebrows which joined together over his nose. His eyes were black, his lips thick. As for his clothing, he went around dressed like a gentile. He wore riding breeches and boots, a short jacket and a Polish hat with a leather visor which he pulled down in the back until it touched the nape of his neck. He carved whistles from twigs and he also played the fiddle. Another of his hobbies was pigeons and he'd built a coop on top of Reb Bunim's house and occasionally he'd be seen scampering up to the roof to exercise the birds with a long stick. Although he had a room of his own and a perfectly adequate bench-bed, he preferred to sleep in the hay loft, and when he was in the mood he was capable of sleeping for fourteen hours at a stretch. Once there had been so bad a fire in Kreshev that the people had decided to flee the town. At Reb Bunim's house everyone had been looking for Mendel so that he might help pack and carry things away. But there had been no Mendel to be found anywhere. Only after the fire had been put out at last and the excitement had died down had he been discovered in the courtyard snoring under an apple tree as if nothing had happened.

But Mendel the Coachman wasn't only a sleeper. It was well-known that he chased the women. One thing, however, could be said for him: he didn't go after the Kreshev maidens.

His escapades were always with young peasant girls from the neighboring villages. The attraction that he had for these women seemed almost unnatural. The beer drinkers at the local tavern maintained that Mendel had only to gaze at one of these girls and she would immediately come to him. It was known that more than one had visited him in his attic. Naturally the peasants didn't like this and Mendel had been warned that one of these days they would chop off his head, but he ignored these threats and wallowed deeper and deeper in carnality. There wasn't a village that he had visited with Reb Bunim where he didn't have his "wives" and families. It almost seemed true that a whistle from him was sufficient sorcery to bring some girl flying to his side. Mendel, however, didn't discuss his power over women. He drank no whiskey, avoided fights, and stayed away from the shoemakers, tailors, hoopers and brushmakers that comprised the poorer population of Kreshev. Nor did they regard him as one of them. He didn't even bother much about money. Reb Bunim, it was said, supplied him with room and board only. But when a Kreshev teamster wanted to hire him and pay him real wages, Mendel remained loyal to the house of Reb Bunim. He apparently did not mind being a slave. His horses and his boots, his pigeons and his girls were the only things that concerned him. So the townspeople gave up on Mendel the Coachman.

"A lost soul," they commented.—"A Jewish gentile."

And gradually they became accustomed to him and then forgot him.

III
THE ARTICLES OF ENGAGEMENT

As soon as Lise turned fifteen, conjecture began about whom she would marry. Shifrah Tammar was sick, and relations between her and Reb Bunim were strained, so Reb Bunim decided to discuss the matter with his daughter. When the subject was mentioned Lise became shy and would reply that she would do what her father thought best.

"You have two possibilities," Reb Bunim said during one of these conversations. "The first is a young man from Lublin who comes of a very wealthy family but is no scholar. The other is from Warsaw and a real prodigy. But I must warn you that he doesn't have a cent. Now speak up, girl. The decision is up to you. Which would you prefer?"

"Oh, money," Lise said scornfully. "What value does it have? Money can be lost, but not knowledge." And she turned her gaze downward.

"Then, if I understand you correctly, you prefer the boy from Warsaw?" Reb Bunim said, stroking his long, black beard.

"You know best, Father. . . ." Lise whispered.

"One thing in addition that I should mention," he went on, "is that the rich man is very handsome—tall and with blond hair. The scholar is extremely short—a full head shorter than you."

Lise grasped both of her braids and her face turned red and then quickly lost all color. She bit her lip.

"Well, what have you decided, daughter?" Reb Bunim demanded. "You mustn't be ashamed to speak."

Lise began to stammer and her knees trembled from shame. "Where is he?" she asked. "I mean, what does he do? Where is he studying?"

"The Warsaw boy? He is, may God preserve us, an orphan, and he is at present studying at the Zusmir Yeshiva. I am told that he knows the entire Talmud by heart and that he is also a philosopher and a student of the cabala. He has already written a commentary on Maimonides, I believe."

"Yes," Lise mumbled.

"Does that mean that you want him?"

"Only if you approve, Father."

And she covered her face with both of her hands and ran from the room. Reb Bunim followed her with his eyes. She delighted him—her beauty, chastity, intelligence. She was closer to him than to her mother, and although almost fully grown, would cuddle close to him and run her fingers through his beard. Fridays before he went off to the bath house she would have a clean shirt ready for him and on his return before the lighting of the candles she would serve him freshly-baked cake and plum stew. He never heard her laughing raucously as did the other young girls nor did she ever go barefoot in his presence. After the Sabbath meal when he napped, she would walk on tiptoe so as not to wake him. When he was ill, she would put her hand on his forehead to see whether he had fever and would bring all sorts of medicine and tidbits. On more than one occasion Reb Bunim had envied the happy young man who would have her as a wife.

Some days later the people of Kreshev learned that Lise's prospective husband had arrived in town. The young man came in a wagon by himself and he stayed at the house of Rabbi Ozer. Everyone was surprised to see what a scrawny fellow he was, small and thin, with black tousled sidelocks, a pale face and a pointed chin which was barely covered by a few sparse whiskers. His long gabardine reached to below the ankles. His back was bent and he walked rapidly and as if he didn't know where he was going. The young girls crowded to the windows and watched him pass by. When he arrived at the study house, the men came up to greet him and he immediately began to expatiate in the cleverest possible way. There was no mistaking that this man was a born city dweller.

"Well, you really have some metropolis here," the young man observed.

"No one's claiming that it's Warsaw," one of the town boys commented.

The young cosmopolitan smiled.

"One place is pretty much like another," he pointed out. "If they're on the face of the earth, they're all the same."

This said, he began to quote liberally from the Babylonian Talmud and the Talmud of Jerusalem, and when he was finished with that he entertained everyone with news about what was going on in the great world beyond Kreshev. He wasn't himself personally acquainted with Radziwill but he had seen him and he did know a follower of Sabbatai Zevi, the false Messiah. He also had met a Jew who came from Shushan which was the ancient capital of Persia and another Jew who had become a convert and studied the Talmud in secret. As if this weren't enough, he began to ask those assembled the most difficult of riddles and, when he tired of that, amused himself by repeating anecdotes of Rabbi Heshl. Somehow or other he managed to convey the additional information that he knew how to play chess, could paint murals employing the twelve signs of the zodiac, and write Hebrew verse which could be read either backwards or forwards and said exactly the same thing no matter how you read it. Nor was this all. This young prodigy, in addition, had studied philosophy and the cabala, and was an adept in mystical mathematics, being able even to work out the fractions which are to be found in the treatise of Kilaim. It goes without saying that he had had a look at the Zohar and "The Tree of Life" and he knew "The Guide to the Perplexed" as well as his own first name.

He had come to Kreshev looking ragged, but several days after his arrival Reb Bunim outfitted him in a new gabardine, new shoes and white stockings, and presented him with a gold watch. And now the young man began to comb his beard and curl his sidelocks. It was not until the signing of the contract that Lise saw the bridegroom but she had received reports of how learned he was and she was happy that she had chosen him and not the rich young man from Lublin.

The festivities to celebrate the signing of the Engagement Contract were as noisy as a wedding. Half the town had been invited. As always the men and women were seated separately and Shloimele, the groom-to-be, made an extremely clever speech and then signed his name with a brilliant flourish. Several of the town's most learned men tried to converse with him on weighty subjects, but his rhetoric and wisdom were too much for them. While the celebration was still going on, and before the serving of the banquet, Reb Bunim broke the usual custom that the bride and groom must not meet before the marriage and let Shloimele into Lise's chamber since the true interpretation of the law is that a man not take a wife unless he has seen her. The young man's gabardine was unbuttoned, exposing his silk vest and gold watch chain. He appeared a man of the world with his brightly polished shoes and velvet skull cap perched on the top of his head. There was moisture on his high forehead and his cheeks were flushed. Inquisitively, bashfully, he gazed about him with his dark eyes, and his index finger kept twining itself nervously around a fringe of his sash. Lise turned a deep red when she saw him. She had been told that he was not at all good-looking but to her he seemed handsome. And this was the view of the other girls who were present. Somehow or other Shloimele had become much more attractive.

"This is the girl you are to marry," Reb Bunim said. "There's no need for you to be bashful."

Lise had on a black silk dress and around her neck was a string of pearls which was the present she had been given for this occasion. Her hair appeared almost red under the glow of candlelight, and on the finger of her left hand she wore a ring with the letter "M" inscribed upon it, the first letter of the word *mazeltov*. At the moment of Shloimele's entrance she had been holding an embroidered handkerchief in her hand but upon seeing him it had fallen from her fingers. One of the girls in the room walked over and picked it up.

"It's a very fine evening," Shloimele said to Lise.

"And an excellent summer," answered the bride and her two attendants.

"Perhaps it's a trifle hot," Shloimele observed.

"Yes, it is hot," the three girls answered again in unison.

"Do you think the fault is mine?" Shloimele asked in a sort of singsong. "It is said in the Talmud. . . ."

But Shloimele didn't get any further as Lise interrupted him.

"I know very well what the Talmud says. 'A donkey is cold even in the month of Tammuz.' "

"Oh, a Talmudic scholar!" Shloimele exclaimed in surprise, and the tips of his ears reddened.

Very soon after that the conversation ended and everyone began to crowd into the room. But Rabbi Ozer did not approve of the bride and groom meeting before the wedding, and he ordered them to be separated. So Shloimele was once more surrounded only by men and the celebration continued until daybreak.

IV
LOVE

From the very first moment that she saw him Lise loved Shloimele deeply. At times she believed that his face had been shown to her in a dream before the marriage. At other times she was certain that they had been married before in some other existence. The truth was that I, the Evil Spirit, required so great a love for the furtherance of my schemes.

At night when Lise slept I sought out his spirit and brought it to her and the two of them spoke and kissed and exchanged love tokens. All of her waking thoughts were of him. She held his image within her and addressed it, and this fiction within her replied to her words. She bared her soul to it, and it consoled her and uttered the words of love that she longed to hear. When she put on a dress or a nightgown she imagined that Shloimele was present, and she felt shy and was pleased that her skin was pale and smooth. Occasionally she would ask this apparition those questions which had baffled her since childhood: "Shloimele, what is the sky? How deep is the earth? Why is it hot in summer and cold in the winter? Why do corpses gather at night to pray in the synagogue? How can one see a demon? Why does one see one's reflection in a mirror?"

And she even imagined that Shloimele answered each of these questions. There was one other question that she asked the shadow in her mind: "Shloimele, do you really love me?"

Shloimele reassured her that no other girl was equal to her in beauty. And in her daydreams she saw herself drowning in the river San and Shloimele rescued her. She was abducted by evil spirits and he saved her. Indeed, her mind was all daydreams, so confused had love made her.

But as it happened, Reb Bunim postponed the wedding until the Sabbath after Pentecost and so Lise was forced to wait nearly three quarters of a year longer. Now through her impatience she understood what misery Jacob had undergone when he had been forced to wait seven years before marrying Rachel. Shloimele remained at the Rabbi's house and would not be able to visit Lise again until Chanukah. The young girl often stood at the window in a vain attempt to catch a glimpse of him, for the path from the Rabbi's to the study house did not pass Reb Bunim's. The only news that Lise received of him was from the girls who came to see her. One reported that he had grown slightly taller and another said that he was studying the Talmud with the other young men at the study house. A third girl observed that obviously the Rabbi's wife was not feeding Shloimele properly as he had become quite thin. But out of modesty Lise refrained from questioning her friends too closely; nevertheless she blushed each time her beloved's name was mentioned. In order to make the winter pass more quickly she began to embroider for her husband-to-be a phylactery bag and a cloth to cover the Sabbath loaf. The bag was of black velvet upon which she sewed in gold thread a star of David along with Shloimele's name and the date of the month and year. She took even greater pains with the tablecloth on which were stitched two loaves of bread and a goblet. The words "Holy Sabbath" were done in silver thread, and in the four corners the heads of a stag, a lion, a leopard, and an eagle were embroidered. Nor did she forget to line the seams of the cloth with beads of various colors and she decorated the edges with fringes and tassels. The girls of Kreshev were overwhelmed by her skill and begged to copy the pattern she had used.

Her engagement had altered Lise: she had become even more beautiful. Her skin was white and delicate; her eyes gazed off into space. She moved through the house with the silent step of a somnambulist. From time to time she would smile for no reason at all, and she would stand in front of the mirror for hours on end, arranging her hair and speaking to her reflection as though she had been bewitched. Now if a beggar came to the house she received him graciously and gladly offered him alms. After every meal she went to the poorhouse, bringing soup and meat to the ill and indigent. The poor unfortunates would smile and bless her: "May God grant that you soon eat soup at your wedding."

And Lise quietly added her own "Amen."

Since time continued to hang heavy on her hands, she often browsed among the books in her father's library. There she came across one entitled "The Customs of Marriage" in which it was stated that the bride must purify herself before the ceremony, keep track of her periods and attend the ritual bath. The book also enumerated the wedding rites, told of the period of the seven nuptial benedictions, admonished husband and wife on their proper conduct, paying particular attention to the woman and setting forth a myriad of details. Lise found all of this very interesting since she already had some idea of what went on between the sexes and had even witnessed the love-play of birds and animals. She began to meditate carefully on what she had read, and spent several sleepless nights deep in thought. Her modesty became more intense than it had ever been before, and her face grew flushed and she became feverish; her behavior was so strange that the servant thought she had been bewitched by the evil eye, and sang incantations to cure her. Every time the name of Shloimele was mentioned, she blushed—whether she was included in the reference or not; and whenever anyone approached, she concealed the book of instructions she was forever reading. What was more, she became anxious and suspicious and soon she had got herself into such a state that she both looked forward to the day of marriage and turned away in dread. But Shifrah Tammar just went on preparing her daughter's trousseau. Though estranged from her daughter, she nevertheless wanted the wedding to be so magnificent that the event would live on for years in the minds of the people of Kreshev.

V
THE WEDDING

The wedding was indeed a grand one. Dressmakers from Lublin had made the bride's garments. For weeks there had been seamstresses at Reb Bunim's house, embroidering and stitching lace on nightgowns, lingerie, and shirtwaists. Lise's wedding gown had been made of white satin and its train was a full four cubits in length. As for food, the cooks had baked a Sabbath loaf which was almost the size of a man and was braided at both ends. Never before had such a bread been seen in Kreshev. Reb Bunim had spared no expense; at his order, sheep, calves, hens, geese, ducks, capons had been slaughtered for the wedding feast. There was also fish from the river San and Hungarian wines and mead supplied by the local innkeeper. The day of the wedding Reb Bunim commanded that the poor of Kreshev be fed, and when word got around an assortment of riffraff from the neighboring district drifted into town to surfeit themselves also. Tables and benches were set up in the street and the beggars were served white Sabbath loaves, stuffed carp, meat stewed in vinegar, gingerbread and tankards of ale. Musicians played for the vagrants and the traditional wedding jester entertained them. The tattered multitude formed circles in the center of the market place and danced and jigged delightedly. Everyone was singing and bellowing and the noise was deafening. At evening, the wedding guests began to assemble at Reb Bunim's house. The women wore beaded jackets, headbands, furs, all of their jewelry. The girls had on silk dresses and pointed shoes made especially for the occasion, but inevitably the dressmakers and cobblers had been unable to fill all orders and there were quarrels. There was more than one girl who stayed home, huddling close to the stove the night of the wedding and, unlucky one, weeping her eyes out.

That day Lise fasted and when it was prayer time confessed her sins. She beat her breast as though it were the Day of Atonement for she knew that on one's wedding day all one's transgressions are forgiven. Although she was not particularly pious, and at time even wavered in her faith, as is common with those who are reflective, on this occasion she prayed with great fervor. She also offered up prayers for the man who by the end of the day would have become her husband. When Shifrah Tammar came into the room and saw her daughter standing in a corner with tears in her eyes and beating herself with her fists, she blurted out, "Look at the girl! A real saint!" —and she demanded that Lise stop crying or her eyes would look red and puffy when she stood beneath the canopy.

But you can take my word for it, it was not religious fervor that was causing Lise to weep. For days and weeks before the wedding I had been busy applying myself. All sorts of strange and evil thoughts had been tormenting the girl. One moment she feared that she might not be a virgin at all, and the next she would dream about the instant of deflowering and would burst into tears, fearful that she would not be able to stand the pain. At other times she would be torn by shame, and the very next second would fear that on her wedding night she would perspire unduly, or become sick to her stomach, or wet the bed, or suffer worse humiliation. She also had a suspicion that an enemy had bewitched her, and she searched through her clothing, looking for hidden knots. She wanted to be done with these anxieties but she couldn't control them. "Possibly," she said to herself on one occasion, "I am only dreaming this and I am not to be married at all. Or, perhaps, my husband is some sort of a devil who has materialized in human form and the wedding ceremony will be only a fantasy and the guests, spirits of evil."

This was only one of the nightmares she suffered. She lost her appetite, became constipated, and though she was envied by all the girls in Kreshev, none knew the agony she was undergoing.

Since the bridegroom was an orphan, his father-in-law, Reb Bunim, took care of supplying him with a wardrobe. He ordered for his son-in-law two coats made of fox fur, one for everyday and one for the Sabbath, two gabardines, one of silk and one of satin, a cloth overcoat, a couple of dressing gowns, several pairs of trousers, a thirteen-pointed hat edged with skunk, as well as a Turkish prayer shawl with three ornaments. Included in the gifts to the bridegroom were a silver spice box upon which a picture of the wailing wall was engraved, a golden citron container, a breadknife with a mother-of-pearl handle, a tobacco box with an ivory lid, a silk-bound set of the Talmud, and a prayer book with silver covers. At the bachelor dinner Shloimele spoke brilliantly. First of all he propounded ten questions which seemed to be absolutely basic, and then he answered all ten with a single statement. But after having disposed of these essential questions, he turned around and showed that the questions he had asked were not really questions at all, and the enormous facade of erudition he had erected tumbled to nothing. His audience was left amazed and speechless.

I won't linger too long over the actual ceremony. Suffice it to say that the crowd danced, sang and jumped about the way crowds always do at a wedding, particularly when the richest man in town marries off his daughter. A couple of tailors and shoemakers tried to dance with the serving girls, but were chased away. Several of the guests became drunk and started to jig, shouting "Sabbath, Sabbath." Several of the others sang Yiddish songs which began with words like "What does a poor man cook? Borscht and potatoes . . ." The musicians sawed away on their fiddles, blared with their trumpets, clanged their cymbals, pounded their drums, piped on their flutes and bagpipes. Ancient crones lifted their trains, pushed back their bonnets, and danced, facing each other and clapping hands, but then when their faces almost touched they turned away as if in rage, all of which made the onlookers laugh even more heartily. Shifrah Tammar, despite her usual protestations of bad health (she could scarcely lift her foot from the floor), was recruited by one of the bands of merrymakers and forced to perform both a cossatzke and a scissor dance. As is usual at weddings, I the Arch-Fiend arranged the customary number of jealous spats, displays of vanity and outbursts of wantonness and boasting. When the girls performed the water dance they pulled their skirts up over their ankles as though they were actually wading in the water and the idlers peering in through the windows could not help having their imaginations inflamed. And so anxious was the wedding jester to entertain that he sang countless songs of love for the guests, and corrupted the meaning of Scriptures by interpolating obscenities into the midst of sacred phrases as do the clowns on Purim, and hearing all this, the girls and young matrons clapped their hands and squealed with joy. Suddenly the entertainment was interrupted by a woman's scream. She had lost her brooch and had fainted from anxiety. Though everyone searched high and low, the piece could not be found. A moment later there was more excitement when one of the girls claimed that a young man had pricked her thigh with a needle. This outburst over, it was time for the virtue dance, and while this dance was going on, Shifrah Tammar and the bridesmaids led Lise off to the bridal chamber which was on the ground floor and so heavily draped and curtained that no light could shine through. On their way to the room the women gave her advice on how to conduct herself, and cautioned her not to be afraid when she saw the groom since the first commandments bids us to propagate and multiply. Shortly after that, Reb Bunim and another man escorted the groom to his bride.

Well, this is one instance when I'm not going to satisfy your curiosity and tell you what went on in the wedding chamber. It is enough to say that when Shifrah Tammar entered the room in the morning, she found her daughter hiding under the quilt and too ashamed to speak to her. Shloimele was already out of bed and in his own room. It took a good deal of coaxing before Lise would permit her mother to examine the sheets, and indeed, there was blood on them.

"Mazeltov, daughter," Shifrah Tammar exclaimed. "You are now a woman and share with us all the curse of Eve."

And weeping, she threw her arms about Lise's neck and kissed her.

VI
STRANGE BEHAVIOR

Immediately after the wedding Reb Bunim rode off into the woods to tend to some business, and Shifrah Tammar returned to her sickbed and medicines. The young men at the study house had been of the opinion that once Shloimele was married he would become the head of a Yeshiva and dedicate himself to the affairs of the community, which seemed appropriate for a prodigy who was also the son-in-law of a wealthy man. But Shloimele did no such thing. He turned out to be a stay-at-home. He couldn't seem to get to the morning services on time and as soon as the concluding "On Us" was said, he was out the door and on his way home. Nor did he think of hanging around after evening prayers. The women around town said that Shloimele went to bed right after supper, and there could be no doubt that the green shutter on his bedroom stayed closed until late in the day. There were also reports from Reb Bunim's maid. She said that the young couple carried on in the most scandalous ways. They were always whispering together, telling each other secrets, consulting books together, and calling each other odd nicknames. They also ate from the same dish, drank from the same goblet, and held hands the way young men and women of the Polish aristocracy did. Once the maid had seen Shloimele hitch up Lise with a sash as if she were a dray horse and then proceed to whip her with a twig. Lise had cooperated in this game by simulating the whinny and gait of a mare. Another game the maid had seen them play was one in which the winner pulls the earlobes of the loser, and she swore that they had continued this nonsense until the ears of both of them had been a blood red.

Yes, the couple was in love and each day only increased their passion. When he went off to pray she stood at the window watching him disappear as if he were off on some long journey; and when she retired to the kitchen to prepare some broth or a dish of oat grits, Shloimele tagged along or else he immediately called, demanding that she hurry out. On Sabbath, Lise forgot to pray at the synagogue but stood behind the lattice and watched Shloimele in his prayer shawl going about his devotions at the eastern wall. And he, in turn, would gaze upwards at the women's section to catch a glimpse of her. This display also set vicious tongues wagging, but none of this bothered Reb Bunim who was most gratified to learn how well his daughter and son-in-law got on. Each time he returned from a trip he came bearing presents. But, on the other hand, Shifrah Tammar was very far from pleased.

She did not approve of this eccentric behavior, these whispered words of endearment, these perpetual kisses and caresses. Nothing like this had ever happened in her father's house, nor had she even seen such goings-on among ordinary people. She felt disgraced and began rebuking both Lise and Shloimele. This was a kind of conduct that she could not tolerate.

"No, I won't stand for it," she would complain. "The mere thought of it makes me sick." Or she would cry out suddenly: "Not even the Polish nobility make such an exhibition of themselves."

But Lise knew how to answer her.

"Wasn't Jacob permitted to show his love for Rachel?" the erudite Lise asked her mother. "Didn't Solomon have a thousand wives?"

"Don't you dare to compare yourself to those saints!" Shifrah Tammar shouted back. "You're not fit to mention their names."

Actually, in her youth Shifrah Tammar had not been very strict in her observances but now she watched over her daughter closely and saw to it that she obeyed all the laws of purity, and would even accompany Lise to the ritual bath to make sure that her immersions were conducted in the prescribed manner. Now and again mother and daughter would quarrel on Fridays nights because Lise was late lighting the candles. After the wedding ceremony the bride had had her hair shaved off and begun wearing the customary silk kerchief, but Shifrah Tammar discovered that Lise's hair had grown back and that she would often sit before a mirror now, combing and braiding her curling locks. Shifrah Tammar also exchanged sharp words with her son-in-law. She was displeased that he went so seldom to the study house and spent his time strolling through orchards and fields. Then it became apparent that he had a taste for food and was extremely lazy. He wanted stuffed derma with fritters daily and he made Lise add honey to his milk. As if this were not enough, he'd have plum stews and seed cookies along with raisins and cherry juice sent to his bedroom. At night when they retired, Lise would lock and bolt the bedroom door and Shifrah Tammar would hear the young couple laughing. Once she thought she heard the pair running barefoot across the floor; plaster fell from the ceiling; the chandeliers trembled. Shifrah Tammar had been forced to send a maid upstairs to knock on the door and bid the young lovers be quiet.

Shifrah Tammar's wish had been that Lise would become pregnant quickly and endure the agonies of labor. She had hoped that when Lise became a mother she would be so busy nursing the child, changing its diapers, tending it when it became ill, that she would forget her silliness. But months passed and nothing happened. Lise's face grew more wan, and her eyes burned with a strange fire. The gossip in Kreshev was that the couple were studying the cabala together.

"It's all very strange," people whispered to each other. "Something weird is going on there."

And the old women sitting on their porches and darning socks or spinning flax had a perpetually interesting topic of conversation. And they listened sharply with their half-deafened ears and shook their heads in indignation.

VII
SECRETS OF THE CHAMBER

It is now time to reveal the secrets of that bed chamber. There are some for whom it is not enough to satisfy their desires; they must, in addition, utter all sorts of vain words and let their minds wallow in passion. Those who pursue this iniquitous path are inevitably led to melancholy and they enter the Forty-nine Gates of Uncleanliness. The wise men long ago pointed out that everyone knows why a bride steps under the wedding canopy but he who dirties this act through words loses his place in the world to come. The clever Shloimele because of his great learning and his interest in philosophy began to delve more and more into the questions of "he and she." For example, he would suddenly ask while caressing his wife, "Suppose you had chosen that man from Lublin instead of me, do you think you would be lying with him here now?" Such remarks first shocked Lise and she would reply, "But I didn't make that choice. I chose you." Shloimele, however, would not be denied an answer and he would go on talking and proposing even more obscene questions until Lise would finally be forced to admit that if indeed she had picked her husband from Lublin she would unquestionably be lying in his arms and not in those of Shloimele. As if this weren't enough he would also nag her about what she would do if he were to die. "Well," he wanted to know, "would you marry again?" No, no other man could possibly interest her, Lise would insist, but Shloimele would slyly argue with her and through skillful sophistry would undermine her convictions.

"Look, you're still young and attractive. Along would come the matchmaker and shower you with proposals and your father would just not hear of your staying single. So there would be another wedding canopy and another celebration and off you'd be to another marriage bed."

It was useless for Lise to beg him not to talk in such a way since she found the whole subject painful and, in addition, of no value, since it was impossible to foresee the future. No matter what she said, Shloimele continued his sinful words, for they stimulated his passion and at length she grew to enjoy them too, and they were soon spending half their nights whispering questions and answers and wrangling over matters that were beyond anyone's knowledge. So Shloimele wanted to know what she would do if she were shipwrecked on a desert island with only the captain, how she would behave herself if she were among African savages. Suppose she were captured by eunuchs and taken to a sultan's harem, what then? Imagine herself Queen Esther brought before Ahasuerus! And these were only a small part of his imaginings. When she reproached him for being so engrossed in frivolous matters, he undertook the study of cabala with her, the secrets of intimacy between man and woman and the revelation of conjugal union. Found in Reb Bunim's house were books "The Tree of Life," "The Angel Raziel," and still other volumes of the cabala and Shloimele told Lise how Jacob, Rachel, Leah, Bilhah, and Zilpah copulate in the higher world, face to face and rump to rump, and the matings of the Holy Father and the Holy Mother, and there were words in these books that simply seemed profane.

And if this were not enough, Shloimele began to reveal to Lise the powers possessed by evil spirits—that they were not only satans, phantoms, devils, imps, hobgoblins and harpies, but that they also held sway over the higher worlds, as for example Nogah, a blend of sanctity and impurity. He produced alleged evidence that the Evil Host had some connection with the world of emanations, and one could infer from Shloimele's words that Satan and God were two equal powers and that they waged constant combat and neither could defeat the other. Another claim of his was that there was no such thing as a sin, since a sin, just as a good deed, can be either big or small and if it is elevated it rises to great heights. He assured her that it is preferable for a man to commit a sin with fervor, than a good deed without enthusiasm, and that yea and nay, darkness and light, right and left, heaven and hell, sanctity and degradation were all images of the divinity and no matter where one sank one remained in the shadow of the Almighty, for beside His light, nothing else exists. He proffered all this information with such rhetoric and strengthened his argument with so many examples that it was a delight to hear him. Lise's thirst to share his company and absorb such revelations increased. Occasionally she felt that Shloimele was luring her from the path of righteousness. His words terrified her and she no longer felt mistress of herself; her soul seemed captive and she thought only what he wanted her to think. But she hadn't the will to stand up to him and she said to herself: "I will go where he leads no matter what happens." Soon he gained such mastery over her that she obeyed him implicitly. And he ruled her at will. He commanded her to strip naked before him, crawl on all fours like an animal, dance before him, sing melodies that he composed half in Hebrew, half in Yiddish, and she obeyed him.

By this time it is quite obvious that Shloimele was a secret disciple of Sabbatai Zevi. For even though the False Messiah was long dead, secret cults of his followers remained in many lands. They met at fairs and markets, recognized each other through secret signs and thus remained safe from the wrath of the other Jews who would excommunicate them. Many rabbis, teachers, ritual slaughterers and other ostensibly respectable folk were included in this sect. Some of them posed as miracle workers, wandering from town to town passing out amulets into which they had introduced not the sacred name of God but unclean names of dogs and evil spirits, Lilith and Asmodeus as well as the name of Sabbatai Zevi himself. All this they managed with such cunning that only the members of the brotherhood could appreciate their handiwork. It provided them great satisfaction to deceive the pious and create havoc. Thus, one disciple of Sabbatai Zevi arrived at a settlement, announced that he was a thaumaturgist and soon many people came to him with chits upon which they'd written their pleas for advice, their problems and requests. Before the counterfeit miracle worker left town, he played his joke and scattered the notes all over the market place where they were found by the town rogues, causing disgrace to many. Another cultist was a scribe and placed into the phylacteries, not the passages of law on parchment as prescribed, but filth and goat dung as well as a suggestion that the wearer kiss the scribe's behind. Others of the sect tortured themselves, bathed in icy water, rolled in snow in the winter, subjected themselves to poison ivy in the summer and fasted from Sabbath-day to Sabbath-day. But these were depraved as well, they sought to corrupt the principles of the Torah and of the cabala and each of them in his own fashion paid homage to the forces of evil—and Shloimele was one of them.

VIII

SCHLOIMELE AND MENDEL THE COACHMAN

One day, Shifrah Tammar, Lise's mother, died. After the seven days of mourning, Reb Bunim returned to his business affairs and Lise and Shloimele were left to themselves. Having purchased a tract of lumber somewhere in Wolhynia, Reb Bunim maintained horses and oxen there as well as peasants to work them, and, when he left, did not take Mendel the Coachman with him. The youth remained in Kreshev. It was summertime and Shloimele and Lise often rode through the countryside in the carriage with Mendel driving. When Lise was busy, the two men went out alone. The fresh pine scent invigorated Shloimele. Also, he enjoyed bathing in the river San, and Mendel would wait on him after they drove to a spot where the water was shallow, for eventually Shloimele would be master of the entire estate.

Thus they became friends. Mendel was nearly two heads taller than Shloimele, and Shloimele admired the coachman's worldly knowledge. Mendel could swim face-up or -down, tread water, catch a fish in the stream with his bare hands and climb the highest trees by the riverbank. Shloimele was afraid of a single cow, but Mendel would chase a whole herd of cattle and had no fear of bulls. He boasted that he could spend a whole night in a cemetery and spoke of having overpowered bears and wolves which attacked him. He claimed victory over a highwayman who had accosted him. In addition, he could play all sorts of tunes on a fife, imitate a crow's cawing, a woodpecker's pecking, cattle's lowing, sheep's and goat's bleating, cat's mewling, and the chirping of crickets. His stunts amused Shloimele who enjoyed his company. Also he promised to teach Shloimele horseback riding. Even Lise, who used to ignore Mendel, treated him amiably now, sent him on all sorts of errands and offered him honeycake and sweet brandy, for she was a kindly young woman.

Once when the two men were bathing in the river, Shloimele noticed Mendel's physique and admired its masculine attractiveness. His long legs, slim hips, and broad chest all exuded power. After dressing, Shloimele conversed with Mendel who spoke unrestrainedly of his success among the peasant women, bragging of the women he'd had from nearby villages and the many bastards he had sired. He also numbered among his lovers aristocrats, town women, and prostitutes. Shloimele doubted none of this. When he asked Mendel if he had no fear of retribution, the young man asked what could be done to a corpse. He didn't believe in life after death. He went on expressing himself heretically. Then, puckering his lips and whistling shrilly, he scampered agilely up a tree, knocking down cones and birds' nests. While doing this he roared like a lion, so powerfully that the sound carried for miles, echoing from tree to tree as though hundreds of evil spirits responded to his call.

That night Shloimele told Lise everything that had happened. They discussed the incident in such detail that both of them grew aroused. But Shloimele was not equipped to satisfy his wife's passion. His ardor was greater than his capability and they had to content themselves with lewd talk. Suddenly Shloimele blurted: "Tell me the truth, Lise my love, how would you like to go to bed with Mendel the Coachman?"

"God save us, what kind of evil talk is this?" she countered. "Have you lost your mind?"

"Well—? He is a strong and handsome young man—the girls are wild about him. . . ."

"Shame on you!" Lise cried. "You defile your mouth!"

"I love defilement!" Shloimele cried, his eyes ablaze. "I am going all the way over to the side of the Host!"

"Shloimele, I'm afraid for you!" Lise said after a long pause. "You're sinking deeper and deeper!"

"One dares everything!" Shloimele said, his knees trembling. " 'Since this generation cannot become completely pure, let it grow completely impure!' "

Lise seemed to shrink and for a long while she was silent. Shloimele could scarcely tell whether she slept or was thinking.

"Were you serious then?" she asked curiously, her voice muffled.

"Yes, serious."

"And it wouldn't anger you at all?" she demanded.

"No. . . . If it brought you pleasure, it would please me as well. You could tell me about it afterwards."

"You're an infidel!" Lise cried out. "A heretic!"

"Yes, so I am! Elisha the son of Abijah was also a heretic! Whoever looks into the vineyard must suffer the consequences."

"You quote the Talmud in answer to everything—watch out, Shloimele! Be on your guard! You're playing with fire!"

"I love fire! I love a holocaust . . . I would like the whole world to burn and Asmodeus to take over the rule."

"Be still!" Lise cried, "Or I shall scream for help."

"What are you afraid of, foolish one?" Shloimele soothed her. "The thought is not the deed. I study with you, I unfold to you the secrets of the Torah, and you remain naïve. Why do you suppose God ordered Hosea to marry a harlot? Why did King David take Bathsheba from Uriah the Hittite and Abigail from Nabal? Why did he, in his old age, order Abeishag the Shunammite brought to him? The noblest ancients practiced adultery. Sin is cleansing! Ah, Lise love, I wish you would obey every whim of mind. I think only of your happiness. . . . Even while I guide you to the abyss . . . !"

And he embraced her, caressed and kissed her. Lise lay exhausted and confused by his oratory. The bed beneath her vibrated, the walls shook and it seemed to her that she was already swaying in the net that I, the Prince of Darkness, had spread to receive her.

IX
ADONIJAH, THE SON OF HAGITH

Strange events followed. Usually Lise did not see very much of Mendel the Coachman. She paid little attention to him when they did meet. But since the day Shloimele had spoken to her about Mendel, she seemed to run into him everywhere. She'd walk into the kitchen and find him fooling around with the maid. Confronting Lise, he would grow silent. Soon she began to see him everywhere, in the barn, on horseback, riding toward the river San. Erect as a Cossack he sat, disdainful of saddle or reins. Once when Lise needed water and could not find the maid, she took the pitcher and headed for the well. Suddenly, out of nowhere, Mendel the Coachman materialized to help her draw water. One evening as Lise strolled through the meadow (Shloimele happened to be at the study house), the old communal billy goat met her. Lise tried to walk past him, but when she turned off to the right, he blocked her path again. When she turned to the left, he leaped to the left also. At the same time he lowered his pointed horns as if to gore her. Suddenly, rising on his hind legs, he leaned his front legs against her. His eyes were a fiery red, blazing with fury, as if possessed. Lise began to struggle to free herself but he was more powerful than she and almost up-ended her. She screamed and was about to faint when suddenly a loud whistle and the crack of a whip were heard. Mendel the Coachman had come upon them, and seeing the struggle, slashed the billy goat across its back with his whip. The thickly knotted thong almost broke the animal's spine. With a choking bleat, he ran off haphazardly. His legs were thickly tufted, tangled with hair. He resembled a wild beast more than a billy goat. Lise was left stunned. For a while, she stared at Mendel silently. Then she shook herself as if waking from a nightmare and said: "Many thanks."

"Such a stupid goat!" Mendal exclaimed. "If ever I get my hands on him again I'll tear his guts out!"

"What was he after?" Lise asked.

"Who knows? Sometimes goats will attack a person. But they'll always go after a woman, never a man!"

"Why is that?—you must be joking!"

"No, I'm serious. . . . In a village where I went with the

master, there was a billy goat who used to wait for the women as they returned from the ritual bath and attack them. The people asked the rabbi what to do and he ordered the goat slaughtered. . . ."

"Really? Why did he have to be killed?"

"So he could no longer gore the women. . . ."

Lise thanked him again and thought it miraculous that he had come when he did. In his gleaming boots and riding breeches, whip in hand, the young man faced her with knowing and insolent eyes. Lise was uncertain whether to continue her stroll or return home, since by this time she was afraid of the goat and imagined that it plotted revenge. And the young man, as if reading her mind, offered to escort and protect her. He walked behind her like a guard. After a while, Lise decided to return to the house. Her face was burning, and as she sensed Mendel's eyes upon her, her ankles rubbed together and she stumbled. Sparks were dancing in front of her.

Later when Shloimele came home, Lise wanted to tell him everything at once, but she restrained herself. Not until that night after putting out the light, did she tell him. Shloimele's astonishment was boundless and he questioned Lise in detail. He kissed and caressed her and the incident seemed to please him immensely. Suddenly he said: "That damned billy goat wanted you—", and Lise asked: "How could a goat possibly want a woman?" He explained that beauty as great as hers could arouse even a goat. At the same time he praised the coachman for his loyalty and argued that his appearance at the propitious moment had been no accident but a manifestation of love, and that he was ready to go through fire for her. When Lise wondered how Shloimele could know all this, he promised to reveal a secret to her. He directed her to place her hand under his thigh in accordance with ancient custom, imploring her never to reveal a word of this.

When she had obliged him, he began, "Both you and the coachman are reincarnations and descended from a common spiritual source. You, Lise, were in your first existence Abeishag the Shunammite, and he was Adonijah, the son of Haggith. He desired you and sent Bathsheba to King Solomon so that he might surrender you to him for a wife, but since according to the law you were David's widow, his wish was punishable by death and the Horns of the Altar could not protect him, for he was taken away and killed. But law applies only to the body, not the soul. Thus, when one soul lusts for another, the heavens decree that they can find no peace until that lust is gratified. It is written that the Messiah will not come until all passions have been consummated, and because of this, the generations before the Messiah will be completely impure! And when a soul cannot consummate its desire in one existence, it is reincarnated again and again and thus it was with you two. Almost three thousand years now your souls have wandered naked and cannot enter the World of Emanations from where they stem. The forces of Satan have not allowed you two to meet, for then redemption would come. So it happened that when he was a prince, you were a handmaiden, and when you were a princess, he was a slave. In addition, you were separated by oceans. When he sailed to you, the Devil created a storm and sank the ship. There were other obstacles too, and your grief was intense. Now you are both in the same house, but since he is an ignoramus, you shun him. Actually, holy spirits inhabit your bodies, crying out in the dark and longing for union. And you are a married woman because there is a kind of cleansing that can be accomplished through adultery alone. Thus Jacob consorted with two sisters and Jehudah lay with Tamar, his daughter-in-law, and Reuben violated the bed of Bilhah, his own father's concubine and Hosea took a wife from a brothel, and that is how it was with the rest of them. And know also that the goat was no common goat, but a devil, one of Satan's own and if Mendel hadn't come when he did, the beast would have, God forbid, done you injury."

When Lise inquired if he, Shloimele, were also a reincarnation, he said that he was King Solomon and that he'd returned to earth to nullify the error of his earlier existence, that because of the sin of having Adonijah executed, he was not able to enter the Mansion due him in Paradise. When Lise asked what would follow the correction of the error, if they would all then have to leave the earth, Shloimele replied that he and Lise would subsequently enjoy a long life together but he said nothing of Mendel's future, intimating only that the young man's stay on earth would be a short one. And he made all these statements with the dogmatic absoluteness of the cabalist to whom no secret is inviolate.

When Lise heard his words, a tremor shook her and she lay there numbed. Lise, familiar with the Scriptures, had often felt a compassion of Adonijah, King David's errant son, who'd lusted for his father's concubine and wished to be king and paid with his head for his rebelliousness. More than once she had wept with pity on reading this chapter in the Book of Kings. She had also pited Abeishag the Shunammite, the fairest maiden in the land of Israel, who although carnally not known to the king was forced to remain a widow for the rest of her life. It was a revelation to hear that she, Lise, was actually Abeishag the Shunammite and that Adonijah's soul dwelt in Mendel's body.

Suddenly it occurred to her that Mendel indeed resembled Adonijah as she had fancied him in her imagination, and she considered this astonishing. She realized now why his eyes were so black and strange, his hair so thick, why he avoided her and kept himself apart from people and why he gazed at her with such desire. She began to imagine that she could remember her earlier existence as Abeishag the Shunammite and how Adonijah had driven past the palace in a chariot, fifty men running before him, and although she served King Solomon, she'd felt a strong desire to give herself to Adonijah. . . . It was as if Shloimele's explanation had unfolded a deep riddle to her and released within her the skein of secrets long past.

That night, the couple did not sleep. Shloimele lay next to her and they conversed quietly until morning. Lise asked questions and Shloimele answered them all reasonably, for my people are notoriously glib, and in her innocence, she believed everything. Even a cabalist could have been fooled into thinking that these were the words of the living God and that Elijah the Prophet revealed himself to Shloimele. Shloimele's words aroused him to such enthusiasm that he tossed and jerked and his teeth chattered as if he were feverish and the bed swayed beneath him and rivulets of sweat coursed from his body. When Lise realized what she was destined to do, and that Shloimele had to be obeyed, she wept bitterly and soaked her pillow with tears. And Shloimele comforted her and caressed her and divulged to her the innermost secrets of the cabala. At dawn she lay in a stupor, her strength evaporated, more dead than alive. And thus the power of a false cabalist and the corrupt words of a disciple of Sabbatai Zevi caused a modest woman to stray from the path of righteousness.

In truth, Shloimele, the villain, devised this whim merely to satisfy his own depraved passions, since he had grown perverse from too much thinking, and what gratified him would make the average person suffer intensely. From an overabundance of lust he had become impotent. Those who understand the complexities of human nature know that joy and pain, ugliness and beauty, love and hate, mercy and cruelty and other conflicting emotions often blend and cannot be separated from each other. Thus I am able not only to make people turn away from the Creator, but to damage their own bodies, all in the name of some imaginary cause.

X
THE REPENTANCE

That summer was hot and dry. Reaping their meager corn crop, the peasants sang as though they were keening. Corn grew stunted and half-shriveled. I brought in locusts and birds from the other bank of the river San and what the farmers had labored for the insects devoured. Many cows went dry, probably from spells cast by witches. In the village of Lukoff, not far from Kreshev, a witch was seen riding a hoop and brandishing a broom. Before her ran something with black elflocks, a furry hide and a tail. The millers complained that imps scattered devil's dung in their flour. A herder of horses who tended his animals at night near the marshes, saw hovering in the sky a creature with a crown of thorns and Christians considered this an omen that their Day of Judgment was not far off.

It was the month of Elul. A blight struck the leaves which tore loose from the trees and whirled about in circles in the wind. The heat of the sun blended with the frigid breeze from the Congealed Sea. The birds that migrate to distant lands, held a meeting on the rooftop of the synagogue, chirped, twittered and argued in avian language. Bats swooped about at evening and girls feared leaving their homes, for if a bat got tangled in someone's hair, that person would not live out the year. As usual at this season my disciples, the Shades, began to perpetrate their own brand of mischief. Children were struck down by the measles, the pox, diarrhea, croup and rashes, and although the mothers took the usual protections, measured graves and lit memorial candles, their offspring perished. In the prayer house the ram's horn was sounded several times each day. Blowing the ram's horn, is, as is well known, an effort to drive me away, for when I hear the horn I am supposed to imagine that the Messiah is coming and that God, praised be His name, is about to destroy me. But my ears are not that insensitive that I cannot distinguish between the blast of the Great Shofar and the horn of a Kreshev ram. . . .

So you can see I remained alert and arranged a treat for the people of Kreshev that they would not forget in a hurry.

It was during services on a Monday morning. The prayer house was crowded. The sexton was about to take out the Scroll of the Law. He had already turned back the curtain before the Holy Ark and opened the door when suddenly a tumult erupted through the entire chamber. The worshipers stared at the place where the noise had come from. Through the opened doors burst Shloimele. His appearance was shocking. He wore a ragged capote, its lining torn, the lapel ripped as if he were in mourning; he was in stockinged feet as if it were the Ninth day of Ab, and about his hips was a rope instead of a sash. Ashen, his beard was tousled, his sidelocks askew. The worshipers could not believe their eyes. He moved quickly to the copper laver and washed his hands. Then he stepped to the reading desk, struck it and cried out in a trembling voice: "Men! I bear evil tidings! . . . Something terrible has happened." In the suddenly still prayer house, the flames in the memorial candles crackled loudly. Presently as in a forest before a storm, a rustle passed through the crowd. Everyone surged closer to the lectern. Prayer books fell to the floor and no one bothered to pick them up. Youngsters climbed up on benches and tables, upon which lay the sacred prayer books, but no one ordered them off. In the women's section there was a commotion and a scuffling. The women were crowding the grate to see what went on below amongst the menfolk.

The aged rabbi, Reb Ozer, was still amongst the living and ruled his flock with an iron hand. Although he wasn't inclined to interrupt the services, he now turned from his place along the eastern wall where he worshiped in prayer shawl and phylacteries and shouted angrily: "What do you want? Speak up!"

"Men, I am a transgressor! A sinner who causes others to sin. Like Jerobom, the son of Nebat!" Shloimele exclaimed and pounded his breast with his fist. "Know ye that I forced my wife into adultery. I confess to everything, I bare my soul!"

Although he spoke quietly, his voice echoed as if the hall were now empty. Something like laughter emanated from the women's section of the synagogue and then it turned to the kind of low wailing that is heard at the evening prayers on the eve of the Day of Atonement. The men seemed petrified. Many thought Shloimele had lost his reason. Others had already heard gossip. After a while Reb Ozer, who had long suspected that Shloimele was a secret follower of Sabbatai Zevi, raised the prayer shawl from his head with trembling hands and draped it about his shoulders. His face with its patches of white beard and sidelocks became a corpse-like yellow.

"What did you do?" the patriarch asked with a cracked voice full of foreboding. "With whom did your wife commit this adultery?"

"With my father-in-law's coachman, that Mendel. . . . It's all my fault. . . . She did not want to do it, but I persuaded her. . . ."

"You?" Reb Ozer seemed about to charge at Shloimele.

"Yes, Rabbi—I."

Reb Ozer stretched out his arm for a pinch of snuff as if to fortify his wasted spirit, but his hand trembled and the snuff slipped from between his fingers. Knees shaking, he was forced to support himself on a stand.

"Why did you do this thing?" he asked feebly.

"I don't know, Rabbi. . . . Something came over me!" cried Shloimele, and his puny figure seemed to shrink. "I committed a grave error. . . . A grave error!"

"An error?" Reb Ozer demanded and raised one eye. It seemed as if the single eye held a laughter not of this world.

"Yes, an error!" Shloimele said, forlorn, bewildered.

"Oi, *vei*—Jews, a fire rages, a fire from Gehenna!" a man with a pitch-black beard and long, disheveled sidelocks cried suddenly. "Our children are dying because of them! Innocent infants who knew nothing of sin!"

With the mention of children, a lament arose from the women's synagogue. It was the mothers remembering their babies who had perished. Since Kreshev was a small town the news spread quickly and a terrible excitement followed. Women mingled with the men, phylacteries fell to the ground, prayer shawls were torn loose. When the crowd quieted, Shloimele started his confession again. He told how he had joined the ranks of the cult of Sabbatai Zevi while still a boy, how he had studied with his fellow disciples, how he had been taught that an excess of degradation meant greater sanctity and that the more heinous the wickedness the closer the day of redemption.

"Men, I am a traitor to Israel!" he wailed. "A heretic from

sheer perversity and a whoremonger! I secretly desecrated the Sabbath, ate dairy with meat, neglected my prayers, profaned my prayer books and indulged in every possible iniquity. . . . I forced my own wife into adultery! I fooled her into thinking that that bum, Mendel the Coachman, was in truth Adonijah the son of Haggith and that she was Abeishag the Shunammite and that they could obtain salvation only through union . . . ! I even convinced her that, by sinning, she'd commit a good deed! I have trespassed, been faithless, spoken basely, wrought unrighteousness, been presumptuous and counseled evil."

He screamed in a shrill voice and, each time, beat his bosom. "Spit upon me, Jews. . . . Flail me! Tear me to bits! Judge me!" he cried. "Let me pay for my sins with death."

"Jews, I am not the rabbi of Kreshev but of Sodom!" shouted Reb Ozer—"Sodom and Gomorrah!"

"Oi—Satan dances in Kreshev!" wailed the black Jew and clapped his head in both hands, "Satan the Destroyer!"

The man was right. All that day and through the following night I ruled over Kreshev. No one prayed or studied that day, no ram's horn was blown. The frogs in the marshes croaked: "Unclean! Unclean! Unclean!" Crows heralded evil tidings. The community goat went berserk and attacked a woman returning from the ritual bath. In every chimney a demon hovered. From every woman a hobgoblin spoke. Lise was still in bed when the mob over-ran her house. After shattering the windows with rocks, they stormed her bedroom. When Lise saw the crowds she grew white as the sheet beneath her. She asked to be allowed to dress but they tore the bedding and shredded the silk nightgown from her body, and in such disarray, barefoot and in tatters, her head uncovered, she was dragged off to the house of the rabbi. The young man, Mendel, had just arrived from a village where he had spent several days. Before he even knew what was happening, he was set upon by the butcher boys, tied with ropes, beaten severely and spirited away to the community jail in the anteroom of the synagogue. Since Shloimele had confessed voluntarily, he got away with several facial blows, but of his own free will he stretched out on the threshold of the study house and told everyone who entered or left to spit and walk over him, which is the first penance for the sin of adultery.

XI
THE PUNISHMENT

Late into the night Reb Ozer sat in the chamber of justice with the ritual slaughterer, the trustee, the seven town elders and other esteemed citizens, listening to the sinners' stories. Although the shutters were closed and the door locked, a curious crowd gathered and the beadle had to keep going out to drive them away. It would take too long to tell all about the shame and depravities detailed by Shloimele and Lise. I'll repeat only a few particulars. Although everyone had supposed Lise would weep and protest her innocence, or simply fall into a faint, she maintained her composure. She answered with clarity every question that the rabbi asked her. When she admitted fornicating with the young man, the rabbi asked how it was possible for a good and intelligent Jewish daughter to do such a thing, and she replied that the blame was all hers, she had sinned and was reconciled to any punishment now. "I know that I've forsaken this world and the next," she said, "and there's no hope for me." She said this as calmly as if the entire chain of events had been a common occurrence, thus astonishing everyone. And when the rabbi asked if she were in love with the young man or if she had sinned under duress she replied that she had acted willingly and of her own accord.

"Perhaps an evil spirit bewitched you?" the rabbi suggested. "Or a spell was cast upon you? Or some dark force compelled you? You could have been in a trance and forgotten the teachings of the Torah and that you were a good Jewish daughter? If this is so—do not deny it!"

But Lise maintained that she knew of no evil spirits, nor demons nor magic nor illusions.

The other men probed further, asked if she'd found knots in her clothing or elflocks in her hair or a yellow stain on the mirror, or a black and blue mark on her body, and she announced that she had encountered nothing. When Shloimele insisted that he had spurred her on and that she was pure of heart, she bowed her head and would neither admit nor deny this. And when the rabbi asked if she regretted her trespasses, she was silent at first, then said: "What's the use of regretting?" and added: "I wish to be judged according to the law —unmercifully." Then she grew silent and it was difficult to get another word out of her.

Mendel confessed that he'd lain with Lise, the daughter of his master, many times; that she'd come to him in his garret and in the garden between the flower beds and that he'd also visited her several times in her own bedroom. Although he had been beaten and his clothing was in shreds, he remained defiant—for as it is written: "Sinners do not repent even at the very gates of Gehenna . . ." and he made uncouth remarks. When one well-respected citizen asked him: "How could you possibly do such a thing?" Mendel snarled: "And why not? She is better than your wife."

At the same time he vilified his inquisitors, called them thieves, gluttons and usurers, claimed that they gave false weight and measure. He also spoke derogatorily of their wives and daughters. He told one worthy that his wife left a trail of refuse behind her; another—that he was too smelly even for his wife, who refused to sleep with him; and made similar observations full of arrogance, mockery and ridicule.

When the rabbi asked him: "Have you no fear? Do you expect to live forever?" he replied that there was no difference between a dead man and a dead horse. The men were so infuriated that they whipped him again and the crowds outside heard his curses while Lise, covering her face with both her hands, sobbed.

Since Shloimele had confessed his sins voluntarily and was prepared to do immediate penance, he was spared and some of the people even addressed him with kindness. Again before the court he related how the disciples of Sabbatai Zevi had ensnarled him in their net when he was a boy and how he had secretly studied their books and manuscripts and come to believe that the deeper one sank in the dregs, the closer one came to the End of Days. And when the rabbi asked why he had not chosen another expression of sin rather than adultery and whether even a man steeped in evil would want his wife defiled, he replied that this particular sin gave him pleasure, that after Lise came to him from the arms of Mendel and they made love, he probed for all the details and this gratified him more than if he had participated in the act himself. When a citizen observed that this was unnatural, Shloimele replied that that was the way it was, all the same. He related that only after she'd lain with Mendel many times and had begun to turn away from him, had he realized that he was losing his beloved wife, and his delight had changed to deep sorrow. He had then tried to change her ways but it was already too late, for she had grown to love the youth, yearned for him and spoke of him day and night. Shloimele also divulged that Lise had given Mendel presents and taken money from her dowry for her lover, who had then bought himself a horse, a saddle and all sorts of trappings. And one day, Lise had told him that Mendel had advised her to divorce her husband and suggested that the two of them flee to a foreign land. Shloimele had still more to reveal. He said that before the affair, Lise had always been truthful, but afterwards, she began to protect herself with all sorts of lies and deceptions and finally it came to the point where she put off telling Shloimele about being with Mendel. This statement provoked argument and even violence. The citizens were shocked at these revelations; it was difficult to conceive how so small a town as Kreshev could hide such scandalous actions. Many members of the community were afraid the whole town would suffer God's vengeance and that, Heaven forbid, there would be drought, a Tartar attack, or a flood. The rabbi announced that he would decree a general fast immediately.

Afraid that the townspeople might attack the sinners, or even shed blood, the rabbi and town elders kept Mendel in prison until the following day. Lise, in custody of the women of the Burial Society, was led to the almshouse and locked in a separate room for her own safety. Shloimele remained at the rabbi's house. Refusing to lie in bed, he stretched out on the woodshed floor. Having consulted the elders, the rabbi gave his verdict. The sinners would be led through the town the following day to exemplify the humiliation of those who have forsaken God. Shloimele would then be divorced from Lise, who according to the law was now forbidden to him. Nor would she be permitted to marry Mendel the Coachman.

Sentence was executed very early the next morning. Men, women, boys and girls began to assemble in the synagogue courtyard. Truant children climbed to the roof of the study house and the balcony of the women's synagogue in order to see better. Pranksters brought stepladders and stilts. Despite the beadle's warning that the spectacle was to be watched gravely, without jostling or mirth, there was no end of clowning. Although this was their busy pre-holiday season, seamstresses left their work to gloat over the downfall of a daughter of the rich. Tailors, cobblers, barrelmakers and hog-bristle combers clustered about, joked, nudged each other and flirted with the women. In the manner of funeral guests, respectable girls draped shawls about their heads. Women wore double aprons, one before, one behind, as if they were present at the exorcizing of a dybbuk or participating in a levirate marriage ceremony. Merchants closed their shops, artisans left their workbenches. Even the gentiles came to see the Jews punish their sinners. All eyes were fixed upon the old synagogue from which the sinners would be led to suffer public shame.

The oaken door swung open, accompanied by a humming from the spectators. The butchers led out Mendel—with tied hands, a tattered jacket and the lining of a skullcap on his head. A bruise discolored his forehead. A dark stubble covered his unshaven chin. Arrogantly, he faced the mob and puckered his lips as if to whistle. The butchers held him fast by the elbows for he had already attempted to escape. Catcalls greeted him. Although Shloimele had repented willingly and been spared by the tribunal, he demanded that his punishment be the same as the others. Whistling, shouting and laughter arose when he appeared. He had changed beyond recognition. His face was dead-white. Instead of a gabardine, a fringed garment and trousers—bits of rag hung from him. One cheek was swollen. Shoeless, holes in his stockings, his bare toes showed. They placed him beside Mendel, and he stood there, bent and stiff as a scarecrow. Many women began to weep at the spectacle as if lamenting one who had died. Some complained that the town elders were cruel and that if

Reb Bunim were around such a thing could never take place.

Lise did not appear for a long time. The mob's great curiosity about her caused a terrible crush. Women, in the excitement, lost their headbands. When Lise appeared in the doorway escorted by the Burial Society women, the crowd seemed to freeze. A cry was torn from every throat. Lise's attire had not been altered—but a pudding-pot sat upon her head, around her neck hung a necklace of garlic cloves and a dead goose; in one hand she held a broom, in the other a goose-wing duster. Her loins were girdled by a rope of straw. It was plain that the ladies of the Burial Society had toiled with diligence to cause the daughter of a noble and wealthy home to suffer the highest degree of shame and degradation. According to the sentence the sinners were to be led through all the streets in town, to halt before each house where every man and woman was to spit and heap abuse upon them. The procession began at the house of the rabbi and worked its way down to the homes of the lowest members of the community. Many feared that Lise would collapse and spoil their fun but she was apparently determined to accept her punishment in all its bitterness.

For Kreshev it was like the Feast of Omer in the middle of the month of Elul. Armed with pine cones, bows and arrows, the Cheder boys brought food from home, ran wild, screamed and bleated like goats all day. Housewives let their stoves grow cold, the study house was empty. Even the ailing and indigent almshouse occupants came out to attend the Black Feast.

Women whose children were sick or those who still observed the seven days of mourning ran outside their houses to berate the sinners with cries, laments, oaths and clenched fists. Being afraid of Mendel the Coachman who could easily exact revenge, and feeling no real hatred against Shloimele, whom they considered addled, they expressed their fury on Lise. Although the beadle had warned against violence, some of the women pinched and mishandled her. One woman doused her with a bucket of slops, another pelted her with chicken entrails and she was splattered with all sorts of slime. Because Lise had told the story of the goat and it had made her think of Mendel, town wags had snared the goat and with it in tow followed the procession. Some people whistled, others sang mocking songs. Lise was called: "Harlot, whore, strumpet, wanton, tart, streetwalker, stupid ass, doxie, bitch," and similar names. Fiddlers, a drummer, and a cymbalist played a wedding march alongside the procession. One of the young men, pretending to be the wedding jester, declaimed verses, ribald and profane. The women who escorted Lise tried to humor and comfort her, for this march was her atonement and by repenting she could regain her decency—but she made no response. No one saw her shed a single tear. Nor did she loose her hold on the broom and duster. To Mendel's credit, let me state that he did not oppose his tormentors either. Silently, making no reply to all the abuse, he walked on. As for Shloimele, from the faces he made, it was hard to tell whether he laughed or cried. He walked unsteadily, constantly stopping, until he was pushed and had to go on. He began to limp. Since he had only made others sin, but had not done so himself, he was soon allowed to drop out. A guard accompanied him for protection. Mendel was returned to prison that night. At the rabbi's house, Lise and Shloimele were divorced. When Lise raised both her hands and Shloimele placed the Bill of Divorcement in them, the women lamented. Men had tears in their eyes. Then Lise was led back to her father's house in the company of the women of the Burial Society.

XII
THE DESTRUCTION OF KRESHEV

That night a gale blew as if (as the saying goes) seven witches had hanged themselves. Actually, only one young woman hanged herself—Lise. When the old servant came into her mistress' room in the morning, she found an empty bed. She waited, thinking that Lise was attending to her personal needs, but after a long time had gone by without Lise appearing, the maid went looking for her. She soon found Lise in the attic—hanging from a rope with nothing on her head, barefoot and in her nightgown. She had already grown cold.

The town was shocked. The same women who the day previous had thrown stones at Lise and expressed indignation over her mild punishment, wailed now that the community elders had killed a decent Jewish daughter. The men split into two factions. The first faction said that Lise had already paid for her transgressions and that her body should be buried in the cemetery beside her mother's and considered respectable; the second faction argued that she be buried outside the cemetery proper, behind the fence—like other suicides. Members of the second faction maintained that from everything Lise said and did at the chamber of justice, she had died rebellious and unrepentant. The rabbi and community elders were members of the second faction, and they were the ones who triumphed. She was buried at night, behind the fence, by the light of a lantern. Women sobbed, choking. The noise wakened crows nesting in the graveyard trees and they began to caw. Some of the elders asked Lise for forgiveness. Shards were placed over her eyes, according to custom, and a rod between her fingers, so that when the Messiah came she would be able to dig a tunnel from Kreshev to the Holy Land. Since she was a young woman, Kalman the Leech was summoned to find out if she was pregnant, for it would have been bad luck to bury an unborn child. The gravedigger said what is said at funerals: "The Rock, His work is perfect, for all His ways are judgment: a God of faithfulness and without iniquity, just and right is He." Handfuls of grass were plucked and thrown over shoulders. The attendants each threw a spadeful of earth into the grave. Although Shloimele no longer was Lise's husband, he walked behind the stretcher and said the Kaddish over her grave. After the funeral he flung himself upon the mound of earth and refused to rise and had to be dragged away by force. And although, according to law, he was exempt from observing the seven days of mourning, he retired to his father-in-law's house and observed all the prescribed rites.

During the period of mourning, several of the townspeople came to pray with Shloimele and offer their condolences, but as though he had vowed eternal silence, he made no response. Ragged and threadbare, peering into the Book of Job, he sat on a footstool, his face waxen, his beard and sidelocks disheveled. A candle flickered in a shard of oil. A rag lay soaking in a glass of water. It was for the soul of the deceased, that she might immerse herself therein. The aged servant brought food for Shloimele but he would take no more than a slice of stale bread with salt. After the seven days of mourning, Shloimele, staff in hand and a pack on his back, went into exile. The townspeople trailed him for a while, trying to dissuade him or to make him wait at least until Reb Bunim returned, but he did not speak, merely shook his head and went on until those who had spoken grew weary and turned back. He was never seen again.

Reb Bunim, meanwhile, detained somewhere in Woliny, had been absorbed in business affairs and knew nothing of his misfortune. A few days before Rosh Hashonah he had a peasant with a wagon take him to Kreshev. He carried numerous gifts for his daughter and son-in-law. One night he stopped at an inn. He asked for news of his family, but although everyone knew what had happened, no one had the courage to tell him. They declared they had heard nothing. And when Reb Bunim treated some of them to whiskey and cake, they reluctantly ate and drank, avoiding his eyes as they offered toasts. Reb Bunim was puzzled by so much reticence.

The town seemed abandoned in the morning, when Reb Bunim rode into Kreshev. The residents had actually fled him. Riding to his house, he saw the shutters closed and barred in midday, and he was frightened. He called Lise, Shloimele and Mendel, but no one answered. The maid too had left the house and lay ill at the Almshouse. Finally an old woman appeared from nowhere and told Reb Bunim the terrible news.

"Ah, there is no Lise anymore!" the old woman cried, wringing her hands.

"When did she die?" Reb Bunim asked, his face white and frowning.

She named the day.

"And where is Shloimele?"

"Gone into exile!" the woman said. "Immediately after the seventh day of mourning. . . ."

"Praised be the true Judge!" Reb Bunim offered the benediction for the dead. And he added the sentence from the Book of Job: " 'Naked I came from my mother's womb and naked I will return therein."

He went to his room, tore a rent in his lapel, removed his boots and seated himself on the floor. The old woman brought bread, a hard-boiled egg and a bit of ash, as the law decrees. Gradually she explained to him that his only daughter hadn't died a natural death but had hanged herself. She also explained the reason for her suicide. But Reb Bunim was not shattered by the information for he was a God-fearing man and accepted whatever punishment came from above, as it is written: "Man is obliged to be grateful for the bad as well as the good," and he maintained his faith and held no resentment against the Lord of the Universe.

On Rosh Hashonah Reb Bunim prayed at the prayer house and chanted his prayers vigorously. Afterwards he ate the holiday meal alone. A maid served him the head of a sheep, apples with honey and a carrot, and he chewed and swayed and sang the table chants. I, the Evil Spirit, tried to tempt the grief-stricken father from the path of righteousness and to fill his spirit with melancholy, for that is the purpose for which the Creator sent me down to earth. But Reb Bunim ignored me and fulfilled the phrase from the proverb: "Thou shalt not answer the fool according to his foolishness." Instead of disputing with me, he studied and prayed, and soon after the Day of Atonement began to construct a Sukkoth booth, and thus occupied his time with the Torah and holy deeds. It is known that I have power only over those who question the ways of God, not those who do holy deeds. And so the holy days passed. He also asked that Mendel the Coachman be released from prison so that he might go his own way. Thus Reb Bunim left the town like the saint of whom it is written: "When a saint leaves town, gone is its beauty, its splendor, its glory."

Immediately after the holidays, Reb Bunim sold his house and other possessions for a pittance and left Kreshev, because the town reminded him too much of his misfortune. The rabbi and everyone else accompanied him to the road and he left a sum for the study house, the poorhouse and for other charitable purposes.

Mendel the Coachman lingered for a while in neighboring villages. The Kreshev peddlers spoke of how the peasants feared him and of how often he quarreled with them. Some said he had become a horse thief, others a highwayman. There was gossip also that he had visited Lise's grave; his boot marks were discovered in the sand. There were other stories about him. Some people feared that he would exact revenge upon the town—and they were correct. One night a fire broke out. It started in several places at once and despite the rain, flames leaped from house to house until nearly three-quarters of Kreshev was destroyed. The community goat lost its life also. Witnesses swore that Mendel the Coachman had started the fire. Since it was bitter cold at the time and many people were left without a roof over their heads, quite a few fell ill, a plague followed, men, women and children perished, and Kreshev was truly destroyed. To this day the town has remained small and poor; it has never been rebuilt to its former size. And this was all because of a sin committed by a husband, a wife, and a coachman. And although it is not customary among Jews to make supplications over the grave of a suicide, the young women who came to visit their parents' graves often stretched out on the mound of earth behind the fence and wept and offered prayers, not only for themselves and their families, but for the soul of the fallen Lise, daughter of Shifrah Tammar. And the custom remains to this day.

Translated by
Elaine Gottlieb and
June Ruth Flaum